YOUNGER GUN

Cawthorne was slow to react. By the time he'd swung his rifle in Givens's direction, Givens had slicked his gun from its holster and was ready to fire on the old lawman. But he hadn't counted on Fargo. Orange flame exploded from Fargo's Colt. There was a roar as one of the other three gunnies drew down on Fargo in the same instant.

But Fargo was so fast he had time to kill Givens and then throw himself to the ground, where the gunny fired uselessly, trying to hit the man who was rolling along the sidewalk. He was so intent on killing Fargo that he left himself open for the Trailsman to fire back at him. Fargo had much better luck than the gunny had. Fargo's bullets split the man's forehead into two pieces.

The other two gunnies were now disinclined to get involved in the shoot-out . . . .

THE TRAILSMAN

#318

NEVADA
NEMESIS

by

Jon Sharpe

A SIGNET BOOK

SIGNET
Published by New American Library, a division of
Penguin Group (USA) Inc., 375 Hudson Street,
New York, New York 10014, USA
Penguin Group (Canada), 90 Eglinton Avenue East, Suite 700, Toronto,
Ontario M4P 2Y3, Canada (a division of Pearson Penguin Canada Inc.)
Penguin Books Ltd., 80 Strand, London WC2R 0RL, England
Penguin Ireland, 25 St. Stephen's Green, Dublin 2,
Ireland (a division of Penguin Books Ltd.)
Penguin Group (Australia), 250 Camberwell Road, Camberwell, Victoria 3124,
Australia (a division of Pearson Australia Group Pty. Ltd.)
Penguin Books India Pvt. Ltd., 11 Community Centre, Panchsheel Park,
New Delhi - 110 017, India
Penguin Group (NZ), 67 Apollo Drive, Rosedale, North Shore 0632,
New Zealand (a division of Pearson New Zealand Ltd.)
Penguin Books (South Africa) (Pty.) Ltd., 24 Sturdee Avenue,
Rosebank, Johannesburg 2196, South Africa

Penguin Books Ltd., Registered Offices:
80 Strand, London WC2R 0RL, England

First published by Signet, an imprint of New American Library,
a division of Penguin Group (USA) Inc.

First Printing, April 2008
10 9 8 7 6 5 4 3 2 1

The first chapter of this book previously appeared in *Mountain Mystery*, the three
hundred seventeenth volume in this series.

Copyright © Penguin Group (USA) Inc., 2008
All rights reserved

 REGISTERED TRADEMARK—MARCA REGISTRADA

Printed in the United States of America

PUBLISHER'S NOTE
This is a work of fiction. Names, characters, places, and incidents either are the
product of the author's imagination or are used fictitiously, and any resemblance
to actual persons, living or dead, business establishments, events, or locales is
entirely coincidental.

The publisher does not have any control over and does not assume any respon-
sibility for author or third-party Web sites or their content.

The Trailsman

Beginnings . . . they bend the tree and they mark the man. Skye Fargo was born when he was eighteen. Terror was his midwife, vengeance his first cry. Killing spawned Skye Fargo, ruthless, cold-blooded murder. Out of the acrid smoke of gunpowder still hanging in the air, he rose, cried out a promise never forgotten.

The Trailsman they began to call him all across the West: searcher, scout, hunter, the man who could see where others only looked, his skills for hire but not his soul, the man who lived each day to the fullest, yet trailed each tomorrow. Skye Fargo, the Trailsman, the seeker who could take the wildness of a land and the wanting of a woman and make them his own.

Nevada, 1867—sometimes man can't tell the difference between friend and enemy. A dark and dangerous time.

1

Skye Fargo's lake blue eyes narrowed when he first heard the cry. Even his big Ovaro stallion swung its head in the direction of the sound.

Fargo had been curious about the sudden appearance of the buzzards circling just over the sand dune ahead of him. The cry lent urgency to his curiosity. Much as he didn't want to, he pressed his stallion to move quickly despite the heat that was well over one hundred degrees not long after dawn. He'd been skirting the edge of the desert for an hour now.

The Ovaro plied the sandy slope with great agility. When Fargo reached the top of the dune, the first thing he saw in the distance was a line of Joshua trees so well-ordered they looked like a miniature windbreak. The land was ragged with the growth of everything from barrel cactus to jumping cholla. And it was alive with creatures ranging from coyotes to scorpions. This was a world unto itself, a world where the piles of seared bones of humans and animals alike testified to the frequency of death.

When he reached the bottom of the dune, he took half a minute to tilt his hat back and wipe his face on his shirt-sleeve. Sweat mixed with dirt had formed a heavy sheen on his face. Beneath the sheen was flesh that had been scorched by too many days in this undying desert where you boiled during the day and froze at night.

So much for the treasure map, Fargo thought ruefully. *And I believed every damned word of it.* Poorer but wiser. That was how the saying went. He sure as hell was poorer

after wasting his time on that map. But any wiser? He grinned to himself. Probably not.

Then he was listening to a new cry, one even louder, even more disturbing. At least it gave him a pretty good idea of where the cries came from.

He didn't see anybody when he reached the Joshua trees but he reined in his horse and dropped to the ground, grabbing his Henry moments later.

He didn't need to go far. His guess had been nearly perfect. Behind the crowded stand of Joshuas, he found a man lying facedown in the sand. He pounded at the ground with both fists and wailed as he did so. Frustration or madness or both? Hard to know without more to go on.

Fargo went over to him. "Roll over if you can."

The man didn't respond at first. But gradually he began the slow process of angling himself up on one hip.

The man looked to be in his early twenties. He was dressed in a blue work shirt and a pair of brown butternuts. He wore inexpensive boots that showed cracks everywhere. An envelope had fallen from the young man's pocket. Fargo picked it up. It was addressed to Bryce Donlon.

The timbre of his moaning told Fargo that Donlon was probably delirious. Inside the moaning Fargo could make out a few words. Fever dreams most likely.

Only now did Fargo see the blood on Donlon's shirt. The wound was pressed against the sand so Fargo couldn't tell how wide the blood had spread. Dark, dried blood. At least it wasn't fresh. At least he wasn't still bleeding.

Fargo bent over to grab the canteen that lay beside the man. He shook it. Then, to make sure, he opened it and turned it upside down. Not even a single drop of water fell to the earth.

Fargo wiped his face again. His eyes stung from sweat and his entire body burned from the heat.

He knelt down next to Donlon. Fargo took his wrist. The pulse was faint but regular. Then he brought his own canteen around and said, "I've got some water for you. You need to drink it."

There was a lot of desert lore. A good deal of it focused on supernatural events. There were numerous stories about men good and bad who haunted the endless, searing sands,

2

and when this youngster's eyes flew open, Fargo knew where some of those myths came from.

The blue eyes belonged to a dead man. Stark, yet uncomprehending. The skin was so sickly it was the color of curdled cream.

"Can you hear me all right?"

But the eyes mirrored no recognition of the Trailsman or his words.

"Can you hear me all right?" Fargo repeated slowly, calmly.

And that was when, without warning of any kind, Donlon sat straight up, his eyes now crazed and focused on Fargo. In a way he had returned from the dead.

Unsettling as hell.

With lips so dry the cracks looked like fissures, Donlon muttered, "You with the posse?"

"Nope. Here, drink a swallow or two of this."

"My sister send you?" The way sweat silvered his face and neck, Fargo suspected that he'd probably just broken a fever. Of course, it was hard to tell when the temperature was this high. Even rolling a smoke could make you sweat harder.

He took the canteen, drank. He handed it back. "I didn't kill her."

"All right. For now I'll believe you."

He glared at Fargo. "But I know you're one of them. One of the posse. You guys shot me in the side but you still don't have me. Not yet you don't."

Fargo realized then that Donlon was suffering not only from his wound but from a nightmare he couldn't escape. His delirium intensified every feeling he had.

"Where's your horse?"

"Dead."

A rustling among the stunted trees. Fargo instinctively went for his gun. Then he smiled when he saw a pert jackrabbit peering warily at him from behind one of the trees.

"That was the last food I had, mister. A jackrabbit. Had to eat it raw. Didn't have no choice."

"You do what you have to, to survive." He nodded toward a shallow, gravelike depression in the sand. "What's this for?"

3

"No blanket, so last night I covered myself with sand. It helps with the cold." The tone of his voice indicated that at least for the moment he'd escaped his delirium.

"So there's a posse after you?"

"Yeah. They say I killed her but I didn't. When I found her, she was dead. I got scared and ran away and people saw me and they thought I was the one who'd stabbed her there in that alley. I ran home but they came after me. My sister wanted me to give myself up but I knew I'd never live to see the trial if I let them take me." He touched the dried blood on his shirt. "They clipped me and it bled a lot but I don't think it's serious. Mostly a flesh wound. I just headed out and the desert seemed like the best place to hide."

Flesh wound or not, Fargo thought, the bullet must have poisoned Donlon somehow. This kind of delirium was often caused by the high fever that accompanies an untreated wound.

"You're not gonna turn me in, are you?"

"No. But I'm hoping you'll turn yourself in."

"You sound like my sister."

"You need food and rest and maybe a doc to look you over. And you're facing a desert crossing. You really think you're up to it?"

"I'd rather face the desert than a lynch rope."

"Maybe so. But maybe you can work something out with the lawman in your town."

"It ain't the sheriff I'm worried about. He's a pretty good man. He's old but he's honest. And he's tough."

"Then why're you afraid of turning yourself in?"

"He's got a deputy named Clyde Rooney who undercuts him. Reports everything he does to Standish and that whole crowd. And it's Standish's daughter, Jane, that I supposedly killed."

"Standish and the sheriff don't get along?"

"Standish and two other men pretty much own the whole valley. You know how men like that are. They expect to get their own way in things. Sheriff Cawthorne, he doesn't do favors like that for anybody. That's what I mean by him being honest."

He had to stop talking, rest. Fargo gave him the canteen

again. "He's one of the few people who'll stand up to them. But Rooney tells Standish everything the sheriff does wrong. Like I said, Cawthorne's old but the people keep reelecting him. But I got to admit, he moves pretty slow for a lawman these days. Standish wants to put his own man in there. Then he'll own everything. Including all the badges."

"I've got some jerky in my saddlebag. Let's get you on your feet and you can at least get something in your belly."

Donlon rose in a lurching, haphazard fashion, so stiff he looked as if he might break in half. But with Fargo's help he managed to climb out of the sand and stand upright without falling over.

Fargo left the canteen with him and then walked over to his saddlebags for jerky and some hard candy he kept wrapped up in a kerchief.

He was just turning back to Donlon when the youngster shouted: "You led them right to me, you bastard!"

At first Fargo had no idea what Donlon was talking about. But when he glanced to his left, he saw them at the crest of the dune. Five of them on horses, each of them with a rifle. One of them had field glasses. By now they would definitely have identified Donlon.

Donlon didn't wait for any explanation. He took off running as well as he could across the unending expanse of sand and brush, into the steamy center of the desert. From what Fargo could hear, Donlon was screaming nonsense. He was not done with delirium yet. Not completely.

He wouldn't get far. He'd collapse before long. But he just might get far enough to give the posse a good excuse to swoop down on him and kill him. At least that's how he'd characterized these men under the sway of the rich man Standish.

Fargo didn't have any choice but to go after him. The way sand sometimes sucked at your boots made speedy progress impossible. In places it was like trying to run in six inches of heavy snow.

But Fargo had a lot more strength and power than Donlon did, so within three minutes he was grabbing the youngster from behind and forcing him to stop.

Donlon was so weak and out of breath he sank to his knees.

"You're so damned worried about them hanging you, kid, you're not thinking straight. You run away like this, you're giving them the legal right to just shoot you down. You won't need a lynch mob."

Donlon raised his face to the sun. Tears silvered his cheeks. He looked like a little boy. "Maybe it'd be easier if I die right here. If I just let 'em shoot me and get it over with."

"Donlon, you've got a murder charge to face. I'm going to stick around and make sure you get a fair shake. I'm going to see you get a doc and some real rest and a lawyer. You say you've got a sister. I'll work with them. Are you understanding me?"

But Donlon didn't have time to answer. The five men with rifles were streaming down the side of the dune, heading as fast as they could for the Trailsman and their suspect.

2

Donlon started to run again but he was so weak that all Fargo had to do was grab him by the shoulder to stop him. "I've already told you, Donlon. You'd just be giving them a legal right to kill you."

As the five riders drew close, Fargo could see that they were all relatively young men, just a few years older than Donlon himself. Meaning that for some of them, being part of a posse would be a lark. Something to brag about in the saloon. The only one wearing a badge was a tall man wearing a fancy blue shirt that looked like something out of a dime novel and a leather vest that bore the outsize star.

He also had a touch of the dramatic in him. He rode just ahead of the other four like a military man fronting his troops. When they got close to Fargo, the man wearing the star held up his arm and everybody halted their animals. "I'm Deputy Rooney and, Donlon, you're under arrest." Then he gave a signal with a twist of his hand and one of the riders jumped down and came running over to where Donlon stood. Or tried to stand. He was obviously about ready to collapse both from exhaustion and fear.

The man had a pair of handcuffs. As soon as Donlon saw them, he twisted around and looked at the scorched desert behind him. He was thinking, in his delirium, that maybe he could make it, that they wouldn't want to follow him into the desert this time of day, with the worst of the heat yet to come.

What Donlon hadn't noticed was that Rooney had his rifle pointed right at his chest. If Donlon tried to run or

even put up much of a fight, Rooney would kill him for sure.

Fargo said, "Don't be stupid, Donlon. Let them put the cuffs on you. You can ride on my horse back to town."

But as he spoke, Fargo saw that another man with another pair of handcuffs had just dropped to the ground. It was clear who he was coming after—Fargo. Now that Donlon had submitted to the cuffs, Rooney's rifle changed positions. His rifle was aimed directly at Fargo.

Fast as Fargo was with a gun, Rooney would still be able to kill him before Fargo could fill his hand. He had to think of an alternative to avoid being cuffed.

The man approaching him was squat and fleshy. He wore a flannel shirt over a pair of bib overalls. These weren't ideal clothes for a day that was headed toward 130 degrees. Apparently only Rooney got to wear the dramatic clothes.

"You just hold still right there," the man said, holding the cuffs up so he could be sure that Fargo saw them. "Rooney, he showed me how to use these here things so they don't pinch. You just don't try nothing. I'll make sure these here things don't pinch. How's that?"

Fargo almost smiled. This poor bastard was scared. Fargo wouldn't have been surprised if he'd literally peed his pants. Like an animal sensing the superior killing power of another animal, the man in the bibs was wary of Fargo, afraid to get much closer. But what choice did he have? If he didn't get closer, how was he going to put the cuffs on?

And he was right to be wary. Right and stupid. He walked right up to him, blocking Rooney's clear shot. If Rooney shot now, he'd put a mighty big hole in the back of Bibs.

He had done exactly what Fargo had wanted him to do.

Fargo seemed to cooperate. He extended his hands, brought them together at the wrists. Extended his arms to make it easy for Bibs to cuff him, and then when Bibs got close enough—Fargo grabbed him so quickly that there was no way Rooney could safely squeeze off a shot. Fargo spun Bibs around, slid a strong arm across his throat. And was now able to draw his Colt, the barrel of which he slammed right into Bibs's temple.

"He's my cousin, you bastard," Rooney said. He sounded

like an eight-year-old, like this was some kind of game they were playing. Not all the fancy shirts in the world could make him seem dangerous. Not whining this way. Of course that wasn't to say he couldn't *become* dangerous. Weak men were the most deadly of all.

"I was going to cooperate with you, Rooney," Fargo said. Bibs squirmed just then. Fargo tightened his grip on the man's throat. Bibs quieted down. "But you rode in here and didn't even ask any questions. You don't know who I am or anything about me but you were going to arrest me anyway. I'd never laid eyes on Donlon till about a half hour ago. He was in pretty bad shape. I was going to help get him back to town so he could turn himself in. He said he was afraid he'd get lynched. At first I figured he was just talking. But now that I've seen you in action I damned well agree with him. You'd fit in fine at the head of a lynch mob."

His grip on Bibs went up another notch. Fargo hoped Rooney could see how red Bibs's face was getting.

Fargo angled his head slightly toward the deputy who stood next to Donlon. The deputy had his gun drawn but he was smart enough to know that any move he made on Fargo would surely get Bibs killed. Maybe, Fargo thought ruefully, Bibs and this man were cousins, too.

"You can kill me, friend, but not before I kill him."

"He's my brother."

"Then pitch your gun over here."

"You're gonna pay for this."

"Your gun."

The man scowled but pitched his six-shooter about two feet from where he stood.

Fargo turned back to Rooney. "I want all your men to throw their guns down. Then I want the other four to ride back to town. You stay here so we can talk. If you don't try anything crazy, you'll get this man back and you'll take Donlon as your prisoner."

Rooney smirked. "You sound like you think you're really in charge here."

"I just want Donlon to get treated fair. Then I'll ride out of your town as soon as I can."

"You might be spendin' a little time in our jail, mister.

9

What you're doin' here is illegal. I'm a sworn officer of the law."

"I'm helping you bring in a prisoner. I'd think that would be in my favor."

Rooney stared at him, trying to discern what kind of man would raise so much hell just to protect somebody he didn't even know. The man with the startling blue eyes looked like a gunny, though, and you could never tell what a gunny was going to do. Probably better to just do what the gunny wanted. That way Eb would still be alive. Eb's brother, Ronald, would never abide his own blood being killed right in front of him, even if they did pick off the gunny at the same time.

"Throw your guns down, men," Rooney said to the riders on either side of him.

"You gonna do what he says?" the swarthy man on the left said. "He's a cheap tramp. You know what people'll say, you follow his orders?"

"You listen to him, Les," Ronald said. "You don't have no brother on the line here."

"Damned right you listen to him," Eb said. He'd been drooling considerably. The drool ran down his front, staining the upper region of his bib overalls. "I got a wife and a little daughter."

"I sure don't like this," said the rider to the right of Rooney. "Some gunny givin' orders this way."

Rooney led by example. He leaned over and let his rifle drop as gently as possible to the ground. Then he carefully lifted his Colt from his holster and did the same with it.

"Your turn," he said to the man on his left.

"They's gonna be laughin' at you at the saloon tonight, Rooney. Laughin' good and hard." But he did likewise.

And then it was the turn of the man to the right of Rooney. You could see in his dark eyes how he was watching for any chance to get a shot at Fargo. But he was so obvious in his would-be craftiness that Fargo said, "Eb's life is on your head. I wouldn't try it."

"We're gonna meet up again."

"I'm looking forward to it. Now drop the guns."

"You heard him," Rooney said.

3

"Doc Renard's back there with him now," Sheriff Cawthorne said when he returned to the front of the building that housed his office and the jail. "He wants to leave him in that little room we have instead of a cell for now. Says he'll probably recover faster in there. That cell's a little chilly, I guess."

Henry Cawthorne looked to be the grandfather everybody wanted—tall, handsome, possessed of gentle, intelligent blue eyes and a mane of white hair. His entire body spoke of reason and kindness. The trouble was that between his arthritis and his slight limp, Fargo could see that true old age had set in. His virility was fading now and sometimes he seemed forgetful.

Rooney said, "I wouldn't worry too much about him, Sheriff." Rooney looked at Fargo and winked. "I mean, he killed a young girl in cold blood."

Cawthorne's expression tightened. "That's what we think, Rooney. That's not what we know."

"Well, it's good enough for Mr. Standish."

Fargo had a glimpse of what had made Cawthorne an effective lawman. Old as he was getting, he was still able to stand tall suddenly, and his white shirt with the star riding on it seemed to swell. The blue eyes narrowed and danced with hellfire. "Who pays your salary, Rooney? The town or Standish?"

"I just meant—"

"You just meant that you run and tell Standish everything that goes on in this office."

Rooney's face burned with embarrassment. He didn't

like being upbraided by this old bastard under any circumstances. But being upbraided in front of strangers was much worse. Rooney had made Fargo answer questions for a half hour, establishing himself as the most powerful man in the sheriff's office. Several times in the course of the questions, he'd demeaned the sheriff just to make it clear that Fargo should take his orders from Rooney and not Cawthorne. And now Rooney looked weak and very much under the thumb of his boss.

"So here's what you tell Standish—that we've got Donlon in handcuffs and leg irons in a little room to himself. And we put him there at the doc's request. And you tell him that Fargo here didn't have anything to do with the killing so I'm letting him go—despite your idea of charging him with 'aiding and abetting a capital crime.' Or whatever that fancy language of yours was. And you can finish up by saying that I'll be getting Donlon a lawyer and that we'll get him ready to stand trial. I'll wire the circuit judge this morning. It may take three weeks to get him here the way he's always busy. Then we'll have a trial."

With that, Rooney grabbed his hat from a nearby peg and quickly exited the front office of the place, leaving Cawthorne and Fargo alone with the wall filled with wanted posters, the two heavy desks that were nearly lost in the clutter of papers and three spittoons that were full to the brim.

Cawthorne went over and sat himself down. For the first time Fargo realized how arthritic the sixty-three-year-old really was. You could see him wince as he lowered his body to the chair.

"Sorry for all your trouble, Mr. Fargo. Rooney likes to put on a show. He thinks that just about everybody needs to be arrested." He laughed, his false teeth clicked as he did so. "He'd have half the town behind bars if I'd let him. I had to step in and stop him from throwing you in one of those cells back there."

"I appreciate that. But he seems pretty sure that Donlon is guilty."

"Well, if I had to bet, I'd bet he's guilty, too. Donlon's been after her to marry him for the last three years. They went to school together. I'm told he used to follow her

around even back then, when they were nine and ten years old. She always liked him in a sisterly way, I guess, but never romantically. Then she announced sometime back that she was going to marry Frank Rhodes and Donlon went a little crazy. Didn't go to work. Spent most of his time in the saloons picking fights with people. Even showed up at Standish's mansion in the middle of the night and tried climbing up a ladder to her bedroom. Standish probably could've gotten away with taking a gun to him but his daughter, Jane, begged him not to. She finally got Donlon calmed down enough to where he sat on the front porch with her and she fed him enough coffee that he pretty much sobered up. Then she told him that she was going to go through with the marriage and Donlon went crazy again. Started shouting at her and threatening her until a couple of the ranch hands ran him off."

"That's still a long way from murder."

"It doesn't end there, Fargo. The next thing that happened is that he went after Frank Rhodes. Saw him in a café eating supper alone and walked right in and knocked him out. He was drunk, of course. Then he waited until Jane got out of choir practice at the church—she never missed those Wednesday nights; she had a beautiful singing voice—and he made some crazy try at kidnapping her. All these people standing on the church steps watching him but he was so drunk he didn't realize he had twenty witnesses standing in full view. Two of the men from church snuck up on him and took his gun away and then ran him in over here. We put him in the jug for the night."

"I see what you mean. A prosecutor wouldn't have a hard time convicting him with those kinds of stories."

"No," Cawthorne said, "I imagine it won't be that hard to get a conviction, whether he's guilty or not."

Fargo was interested in the way the lawman had phrased that last sentence. "So you think there's still a possibility he didn't do it?"

"A possibility. Yes. He wasn't just stuck on her. She was some kind of goddess to him. I don't know if he could destroy her, especially the way she was stabbed. But then he'd been so crazy lately—" The lawman shrugged. "That's why I want there to be a trial. That's the only way we're going to

find out exactly what the hell happened here." He frowned. "Donlon's a decent man when he's sober. He's just about to come into some money for the first time in his life. Uncle left him and his sister quite a bit. But the way he's obsessed with Jane—I should say 'was' obsessed with Jane—"

The door opened and an almost shockingly lovely red-head in a white blouse and blue butternuts walked in. The only thing that spoiled her elegant, freckled face were the smudges under her green eyes. She hadn't slept in some time.

"Afternoon, Grace." The sheriff said to Fargo, "Grace is Donlon's sister."

Grace's gaze assessed Fargo as she spoke. "Are you the man who found my brother?"

"Yes, ma'am."

"You probably saved his life. I really appreciate it."

She turned to Cawthorne. "May I see Bryce?"

"Sure, Grace."

"I'm sure Mr. Standish won't approve of me seeing him."

"The day I start worrying about what Mr. Standish likes or dislikes, I'll turn in my badge."

She smiled briefly at Fargo. "The bravest man in these parts. Fearless."

"Now that's nonsense, Grace, and you know it. No such thing as a fearless person. Am I right, Fargo?"

"Far as I'm concerned you are. About once a day I get scared of something or other."

"Well, you sure seem fearless to me, Sheriff. And I doubt I'm going to change my mind about that, either."

Fargo dusted off his hat and said, "Guess I'll be leaving, too. I'm getting pretty hungry."

"Thanks again for your help, Fargo."

He nodded to the sheriff and then to Grace Donlon. "Nice to meet you."

She nodded. Fargo thought that if she looked this good distraught, imagine what she looked like when her life was settled and calm.

He started toward the door.

There were six of them. They'd positioned themselves directly in front of the sheriff's office. But they'd been care-

ful to stay back several feet and not get close to the hitching post. It was a free country, wasn't it? These six men, all with guns strapped to their hips, all with clear, angry purpose in their eyes, couldn't be accused of inhibiting traffic in any way. They could stand right here if they wanted to, correct?

No doubt of their intention, Fargo thought as he emerged from Cawthorne's office and saw them. With any luck, there'd be no more of them. With any luck, the people of the town would realize that the best way to handle situations like this was to let the law take its course. With any luck, the town leaders would exert whatever influence they had to stop a lynching from taking place.

Fargo smiled to himself. A couple of these men were so drunk they swayed from side to side. Too drunk to tie a hangman's knot. Which was a good thing.

"Who're you?" the bald one said.

"Might ask you the same thing, mister," Fargo said.

"I don't like smart-mouth strangers."

"Well, I don't like a bunch of tinhorn drunks standing in front of a sheriff's office like they mean to do something."

"You must be the sonofabitch that found him."

"I might be. But if you call me that again, I'm gonna take that six-shooter from you and put it in a very uncomfortable place."

"Tell him, Bowersox. He ain't nobody to be afraid of."

"Looks like your friend there wants to see you get your face busted up," Fargo said. "How about you?"

But the bald man had sensed the power—and now anger—in Fargo. He'd lost the confident look in his eyes and his voice wasn't as loud when he said, "We got a right to ask questions."

"Yeah. But you asked it like you were making an accusation, friend. And I don't take to accusations." He glanced at the faces in front of him. Apparently these men didn't have jobs or they'd taken off work for the day. Sobered up, they might be decent workingmen. But liquored up this way, they were bullies. And potentially dangerous.

Fargo said, "My name's Skye Fargo. I brought Donlon in. I don't know anything about Jane Standish being murdered and I don't plan to know. I'm having some grub and

15

then I'm riding out of here. There's a lot of Nevada I haven't seen. Is that enough information for you?"

Fargo could see that the men weren't pacified. They wanted a fight. Every one of them except Bowersox, that was.

Fargo took two steps off the low-plank sidewalk. He walked up to the heavyset man next to Bowersox. "I asked you if that was enough information for you."

"How do we know you weren't in on it with Donlon?"

"That's a pretty stupid idea. I never laid eyes on Donlon till I saw him in the desert."

"Stupid, huh?" The man's breath reeked of whiskey. He also stank like he was a month past his last bath.

The fist that came up fast was blocked with no trouble by Fargo. The heavyset man didn't have the same luck. He wasn't quick enough to stop Fargo from smashing a left into his jaw or a right deep into his belly. Bowersox made a move on Fargo but he wasn't quick enough, either. Fargo cracked an elbow across Bowersox's nose, blood geysering free almost immediately. Bowersox clamped his hand over his face and dropped to his knees.

A pair of Bowersox's men tried to draw their guns but Fargo had already drawn his. "Your call," he said. "Either throw them down or I kill you right here."

A crowd had gathered. This was too good to miss. Some real excitement. All Fargo wanted was to take care of his belly hunger and get the hell out of this town.

The men dropped their six-shooters in the dust. By this time Cawthorne had come out to see what was going on.

Bowersox snapped, "I want you to arrest this man, Sheriff." His words were muffled somewhat because of the kerchief he held to his nose.

"You got a big mouth and a loud one, too, Bowersox. I heard it all from inside. You started it and it looks like Fargo here finished it. Now get the hell out of here before I run you all in."

"We want to take care of Donlon ourselves," one of the other men said. "We don't need no judge to tell us who's innocent and who ain't."

"You heard what I said," Cawthorne said. "Get the hell

out of here. You men should be at work, anyway. You got families to feed."

But Bowersox wanted the last word. "We'll be back, Cawthorne. Don't think we won't."

He would've sounded more dramatic if he hadn't had his blood-soaked kerchief still muffling his words.

They made sure to leave slowly, demonstrating, or so they thought, that they weren't intimidated by the sheriff's demand to clear out. They didn't go far, either. The Aces saloon was less than a half block away on the other side of the street. They all disappeared behind the batwings there.

"Friends of yours?" Fargo laughed.

"Every murder brings 'em out. There was a time when the only law was lynching. I can remember that when I was a boy. Circuit judges only came around every couple months or so and God help you if a mob decided you were the guilty party. They just strung you up, no questions asked. Most of the time they probably got the right man. But not every time. These fellas like to pretend that it's still lynch law. They need a little excitement in their lives so they show up here. They never really try to get the prisoner but they put on a good show, 'specially at night. They bring torches and collect a big crowd, and me and a deputy have to chase them off with shotguns. And then a couple people print letters in the newspaper claiming that I'm on the side of the criminals because I won't turn them over to the mob."

"Sounds exciting. But I'm afraid I'll have to miss it, Sheriff."

The old man sighed. "I half wish I could ride out with you, Fargo. I'm not looking forward to tonight. I'm getting too old for this. And there's always the chance that somebody's gonna get hurt. Any time you put a big crowd together . . ." He nodded to the saloon. "You can figure out how drunk they'll be by tonight. They'll have a good six, seven hours of drinking in their bellies by then."

"They don't go home for supper?"

Cawthorne snorted. "Not on a day like this. They just want to keep beltin' 'em back."

Fargo put out his hand and the men shook. "Good luck

with everything, Sheriff. I hope to be gone in the next hour or so."

"Good to meet you, Fargo."

The business district was two blocks of false fronts. Fargo searched out a café and went inside, sat down at a table in front of a window and ordered the special for the day, which was beef and potatoes and corn. He had coffee right away.

He was just setting into his meal when he felt a presence at his side. He looked up to see Grace Donlon standing there. Her elegant beauty was as startling to him as it had been in the sheriff's office.

"Would you mind if I sat down, Mr. Fargo?"

"I'm afraid not, Miss Donlon. You're just not good-looking enough for me."

She smiled but it was a wan expression that told of anxiety as much as it did enjoyment. She took a chair across from his and said, "You're the only man I know who can save my brother's life."

4

The portrait she painted of her brother, Bryce, was of the boy who'd always gotten in minor trouble both with the law and with many of his neighbors. Grace attributed this to the fact that their parents had died when they were young—a train wreck on their way back home—and that she had raised her little brother without the influence of a man around. A man would've been tougher on him than she had been. She'd done her best but she was just a teenager herself. And so, for the most part, all she could do was to keep chastising him. But she had no real power over him.

Grace said that his love for Jane had made him crazy.

"That was one reason he was always getting in trouble. He'd get so sad about her, he'd get into a fight or he'd get drunk and steal something or insult somebody who had power in this town. The Standishes couldn't stand him. They could never figure out why Jane gave him so much of her time. And that's why I'm so afraid of what they're going to do to him."

" 'They'?"

"The Standishes." She had her own coffee and, as she raised the cup to her lips, he saw how trim and artfully made her wrist was. He was naturally curious about the rest of her, too. She certainly filled out her blouse most attractively, for one thing. "They want vengeance. I don't blame them. I'd want the same thing. But they don't want to wait for the judge. They want to get vengeance with their own hands. Those men in front of the sheriff's office were just a beginning. Tonight the street will be filled with people like them. And I'm afraid for my little brother."

"He's not so little anymore."

"No. Maybe not to you, anyway. But to me he'll always be 'my little brother.' "

"Somebody you want to protect."

"Somebody I want very much to protect."

He set his coffee cup down. "What if he's guilty?"

"He's not guilty."

"So you won't even consider that possibility?"

"No. I won't. Because I know better."

Fargo rolled himself a smoke. "You have any idea who might have killed her then, or why?"

"As a matter of fact there are two other people who might have done it. One is the young man she was seeing before she took up with Frank Rhodes. His name is Ken Ericson. He's a vice president at the bank. He's still bitter that Rhodes came along."

"He might be bitter but what makes you think he might have killed her?"

"Last month we had a little fair here in town. He got her alone and begged her to come back to him. The trouble was they weren't really alone. He was so loud that people heard everything he said. It was very embarrassing for him. And then he lost his temper and said that if Jane didn't come back to him, she'd be sorry."

"I suppose he'd be worth talking to. You said there were two."

"Yes. Beth Conroy. That's Ken's fiancée. She's a very pretty woman but very emotional. She hated Jane. She knew that she'd never really have Ken. A part of him would always be with Jane. Even after she and Ken were married and had children there'd always be—Jane."

"You need a Pinkerton."

"We couldn't afford one. And anyway, there isn't time. It'd take at least two days for him to get here. And the way Standish is stirring things up—"

"You have proof of that?"

"Bowersox and those other men in front of the sheriff's office—they all work for Standish out at the wagon works. I'm sure he gave them the day off so they could come down here and make Cawthorne's life miserable."

Fargo sat back in his chair and let his eyes rest on her

almost perfect face. "I know what you're driving at, Grace. But I'm planning on riding out of here. Like I said, you need a Pinkerton or somebody like that."

"What if they try to lynch him tonight?"

He wished he had a good answer, one that didn't sound so selfish. But he didn't. "I don't know the lay of the land here, Grace. I don't know who's who or what's what. There's the possibility that your brother's guilty. That can't be ruled out."

"You could rule it out if you looked into things."

"I don't have any authority to look into things."

"You'd have authority if the sheriff made you his deputy."

He laughed, knowing what she was about to say. "You talked him into it after I left his office, did you?"

This time her smile was full, radiant. "He said he'd be needing another deputy, anyway. I just happened to mention that I thought you'd make a good one, especially if things got bad tonight. He's an old man and he knows it. And he can't trust Rooney."

Fargo was about to offer more reasons for not getting involved but her mention of Cawthorne had changed his mind. The thought of a man in his condition standing up to a gang of drunken men bent on lawlessness—Fargo couldn't very well let that happen.

"I know you're going to help me," Grace Donlon said.

"You do, huh?"

"Yes, I do."

And damned if she wasn't right.

"You ever think you'd pack a star, Fargo?" Cawthorne said, amused when he pinned the badge on Fargo.

"I've worn it a couple of times before. But it's been a while."

"Grace told me that you were willing to help, you know, askin' questions. You got the rest of the day for that, a good six hours anyway. See what you can find out. The big problem's gonna be tonight, of course."

"No doubt about that."

"You know what you want to do for now?" Cawthorne said, walking around behind his desk and sitting down.

"Well, I think I'll start with Ken Ericson. You know where I can find him?"

"Right down the street. He's the vice president at the bank. I think that's one reason Jane sort of gave up on him. She wasn't much for power and money. Most of the time you'd find her in the church basement, gathering up old clothes for the poor. She wasn't like her old man at all. Power and money didn't seem to interest her much."

"How about Beth Conroy?"

"Two-story brick house about a block from the Methodist church. She fancies herself a painter. She's got a nice inheritance and so she can afford to fancy herself anything she wants to, I guess."

Fargo took the makings from his pocket and rolled a cigarette. "As far as you know, how were Jane and Frank Rhodes getting along?"

The lawman beamed. "Say, you're not bad at this detective business. You must've had some experience."

Fargo didn't want to tell him that he'd helped a wounded Pinkerton man solve a case. More than "helped" actually. It was Fargo who'd finally solved the case. But that would sound too much like bragging. "A little bit here and there, I guess."

"Well, Frank's used to getting his way, that's for sure. I understand that he was able to be real, real nice when he was courting her. But I also understand he was sort of being his old self lately and that Jane had some second thoughts about marrying him."

"That's good to know. I appreciate it."

"No problem, Fargo. The way I see it, we're partners."

Rooney came from the back of the building just then. "Funny old world, Sheriff. About six o'clock this morning when I brought Fargo here in, I was hopin' you'd throw him in a cell back there. Now look. You put a badge on him."

"This shouldn't be any problem for you, Rooney. Fargo knows what I want him to do. He'll stay out of your way and you stay out of his. And you can tell Standish I said that when you report this to him." Cawthorne laughed. "I might see him over to the café at noon. I can tell him myself if you'd like."

22

Rooney glowered at Fargo. "Just as long as he stays out of my way. That's all I care about." And with that, he turned and walked to his office in the back near the cells.

"I made a devil's bargain with Standish over him," Cawthorne said. "He said he'd support me for sheriff if I let him put Rooney on as my deputy. Well, if I had it to do over again, I sure wouldn't put Rooney on. I have to be careful of every word I say if he's around 'cause everything I say gets back to Standish." He grimaced. "But right now, we've got bigger problems than Rooney, I guess."

Fargo got his smoke lighted and walked out onto the sun-seared street.

Outside his hotel room door, Fargo paused. He'd heard a scraping sound coming from inside. His Colt already filled his hand. Even though he'd been in town only a few hours, he'd made enemies. He had to be careful.

With his free hand, he shoved the door inward and rushed across the threshold. You never knew what you were going to find in a situation like this. But usually it wasn't anything as pleasing as the well-rounded rump of a hotel worker. She was making the bed. And when she straightened up and turned around, Fargo saw that her bountiful rump was matched by bountiful breasts and a shy but knowing blue-eyed glance.

"Are you going to shoot me?" she said playfully, nodding to his gun.

He smiled, holstered his Colt. "I don't like to take chances."

Her shyness seemed to have packed up and left on vacation. "Some chances are worth taking." As she spoke she openly assessed him with that blue-eyed gaze of hers. She obviously liked what she saw.

"I guess you're right about that." He came into the room, walked over to his saddlebags. He took a full bag of Bull Durham out and stuck it in his shirt pocket. When he put the saddlebags back on the chair, he felt the heat of the girl close behind him.

"I have a friend who works the other hotel down the street," she said. "She's always tellin' me about all these amorous situations she gets in with all these handsome

young travelers. Me, all I get in this place is old men who're always hacking and coughing and trying to put their greasy paws on me. You're the first real man I've seen since I started here."

She was in his arms the instant he turned to face her, her breasts tantalizing him, her magnificent rump pushing the rest of her into him. His entire body was awake now, every ounce of him wanting, needing, this simple but enticing creature that he was already urging gently to bed.

She wore a plain skirt and a red blouse. As his eager fingers quickly learned, she wore no undergarments. He found her hot, moist center at once. He got even more excited with her sudden excitement. She bucked and wailed as if she were insane. Nice to know she needed him as badly as he needed her.

He managed to unbutton her blouse, letting her enormous breasts spill free. He made her even crazier when his tongue began to tease the huge brown nipples that crested her breasts.

And then she was returning the favor, freeing his manhood from his trousers, gasping a bit at the size of it, then parting her legs wide so that she could guide him in. Deeper and deeper he thrust as she rose to meet him, his hands grasping those sweet buttocks so that he could grind her closer and closer to him until their bodies seemed as one. Sometimes these were the best times of all—the quick, almost impersonal ones. Hell, he didn't even know her name.

He gave up counting the number of times she panted her pleasure climactically, six, seven, eight. She was a wonder and he kept grinding into her to help her sustain her great joy.

And then the joy became his as his whole body bucked and reared when he reached his own pinnacle of excitement. She worked his buttocks so she could get him even deeper into her. And then he collapsed, his face buried in her neck. And they lay that way for a few minutes. Intimate strangers.

He eased off her after a time and put himself back together. There was work to do. But this had been a memorable interlude. That was for sure.

She did the same. In moments, she'd managed to look composed and efficient once again, a perfect employee.

She walked to the door and smiled back at him. "My name's Inez, by the way."

They both had a good laugh about that one. Intimate strangers indeed.

When Fargo was less than ten feet from his hotel, the pleasure he'd felt with Inez quickly disappeared. He saw a large older man in a blue business suit bearing down on him. The way people in the street stared at this man—their expressions part awe, part fear—Fargo figured he knew who this was. He didn't need to be told.

"You're Fargo."

"That I am, Mr. Standish."

They had an audience. Standish didn't seem to care. Maybe he was so angry he didn't even notice. "I'm told that Cawthorne has you going around and asking questions."

"Word travels fast."

Standish was not only big, he was fierce. His facial features were outsize and his bronze-colored eyes blazed with such rage that he likely terrified most of the people who saw it. "I'm telling you that there's no reason to ask questions. I'm telling you that we already know who murdered my daughter. And I'm telling you that I don't want you nosing around in this thing." He jabbed an enormous finger into Fargo's chest. "And one more thing I'm telling you. If you make even the slightest bit of trouble for me in this thing, you'll leave town in a pine box. You understand me?"

But he didn't give Fargo a chance to answer.

He turned and stormed off, leaving Fargo as speechless as the small crowd that had gathered around him.

5

Frank Rhodes's secretary was a fifty-seven-year-old self-described "follower of the faith" who had been inflicted on him the day he'd opened his law office. His father, who'd lent him the money to get established here in town, insisted that Frank have somebody who would "keep his drunken friends away from him." And Dottie Swinnerton was just the person. She was unmarried and had never been burdened with either a sense of humor or an ounce of fear. She couldn't have weighed more than one hundred pounds and she wore woolen clothes year-round for the sake of "modesty." But for all her eccentricities she was one formidable woman.

Dottie was just finishing up a business letter in her cramped but readable penmanship when the door opened and a sour smell made its way into the reception area. The stench was quickly followed by the sight of the shambling, ragged man with the dirty face and the black teeth known as "Skunk." He had a real name, of course, but nobody ever used it and so it was long forgotten. He wore the same city suit he always wore, one so vile it was covered in splotches—hard, shiny splotches—of God alone knew what. Vomit no doubt numbered among the sources of the splotches. As usual, he carried his battered derby in both hands at chest level, like a supplicant, apparently figuring, or hoping, that this display of humility would keep him from being beaten up again. Men reeling out of saloons often made sport of Skunk, sometimes violently.

"I don't see any reason for you to be in this office," Dottie snapped, holding a lacy handkerchief to her nose.

She'd have to open the windows even wider after he'd gone.

"Ma'am, I need to see Mr. Rhodes."

"Stay right there!" she said as he started advancing toward her desk. After he'd frozen in place, she said, "Mr. Rhodes is busy."

"Would it be all right if I wait, ma'am?"

Dottie, sensibly enough, thought of how bad the office would smell if he was allowed to remain in here even two more minutes. "You most certainly may not. Now you turn around and march right out of here, do you hear me?"

Skunk couldn't have looked more injured if she'd assaulted him physically. In her voice was the contempt of all the people who'd ever laughed at him over the years. How could a single voice contain all that scorn and derision, that innate sense that he had no right to exist?

"Did you hear me? Now you march right on out of here before I call the sheriff. You're not allowed inside. In case you've forgotten."

Another sure sign of the hatred he always had to confront. The town council had passed a law that Skunk was not allowed inside of a "respectable business." This included all but the most vile of saloons.

But he knew he'd only get in more trouble if he asked to see Rhodes again. All he could do was kind of doff his hat the way he'd seen people in traveling shows do when they were singing a song. And give his little bow. And leave the office.

He knew he'd be back, of course. If not during business hours, then after them. Frank Rhodes sometimes worked late. And Skunk was damned well going to see Frank Rhodes because Frank Rhodes was going to make him rich—rich relative to how he'd been living, anyway. Rich enough to get out of this hellhole with some new clothes and some money in his pocket.

A good thing he'd been sleeping one off in that alley the other night . . . a good thing he saw what he saw between Rhodes and Jane Standish just before he fell back to his alcohol sleep . . . a good thing what he saw was going to make him rich.

* * *

27

Dottie Swinnerton, from the doorway of his office, said to Frank Rhodes, "Can you smell him?"

Rhodes looked up. "Excuse me, Dottie. What did you say? I'm working on this letter to the statehouse."

"I asked," she said with great distaste, "if you could smell him."

"Smell who?"

"Whom."

"All right. Smell whom?"

"The creature they call Skunk."

"Was he walking by the office, you mean?"

"Not walking by. He was in here. In the reception area."

Rhodes set his pen down, leaned back in his chair. She had just said something that would normally have amused him. The thought of somebody like Skunk walking into range of Dottie was the stuff of great saloon stories. But when she said this he felt his stomach knot. And at first he wasn't quite sure why. His mind seemed to know something that it wasn't making intelligible. Not as yet, anyway.

And then—

When he was done with her there in the alley and looking for the best way to move quickly away, moonlight fell on something stirring nearby. And from those shadows, staggering as always, he saw the shambling figure of Skunk who seemed to be offering—moonlight glinting off the glass—a drink from his pint of rotgut. Rhodes was drunk enough that he wasn't so sure-footed himself. He stumbled as he began to run away, leaving both Jane and Skunk in the alley.

And now—

Only now did he remember the sudden appearance of Skunk the other night. Ridiculously offering the bottle. Standing so close to Jane—

So he'd remembered, Skunk had. Rhodes had been so drunk that much of the scene in the alley was lost to him. Now he thought bitterly, *All I have to do is ask Skunk. He knows what happened there.*

"It'll take a couple of days to air this place out after he's been in here."

But despite her words, Dottie saw that her employer was

suddenly lost to his own thoughts, staring out the sun-glazed window. She explained this to herself by recalling all the mornings lately he'd come in with a hangover. Next only to dancing, Dottie considered the worst sin of all to be drinking alcohol. She blamed this on Jane Standish. As far as Dottie was concerned, Jane had led poor Frank Rhodes along. Jane wanted Frank to be just so and when he wasn't, she began to question whether she should marry him. Women were the source of all sin in the world, Dottie reasoned. So young Frank's moral decay was therefore the fault of Jane.

"Thanks for telling me, Dottie. About Skunk, I mean."

"If he tries to come in again, I'll get the sheriff."

"Good, good," Rhodes said vaguely. She could tell that his mind had already wandered off again.

After Dottie left, Rhodes stood up and walked to the window that looked out on Main Street. The town was prospering as he'd hoped his marriage to Jane would prosper. In his mind they'd gone hand in hand, his prominence as an attorney and businessman, his family life with Jane.

Three hotels, a schoolhouse, two lodge halls. Wagon works, three blacksmiths, liveries, a white-framed Methodist church and a granite Catholic church. And on the bluffs above the town to the east sat three new Victorian mansions bought with the proceeds from the mines that employed half the men of able body.

A railroad would be coming soon, too. . . .

And as he stared preoccupied out his window, a figure came into focus. A figure he at first forbade himself to recognize. But a figure that seemed to have the power to impose itself on his mind whether he wanted it to or not.

The figure was Skunk, dragging himself along the edge of Main Street, filthy even from this distance. Some people stopped to stare at him as if he were some kind of vile supernatural apparition. Others, particularly ladies, scurried away from him as quickly as possible. Whatever contagion he was carrying, they wanted no part of it.

And then he turned away from the window, thinking of the funeral to come the day after tomorrow. Jane Standish, the only woman he'd ever loved, would be buried in the cemetery reserved for the town's elite.

He just wished he could remember what had happened in that alley the other night. . . .

As much as he *needed* to talk to Skunk, he was terrified of what the scabrous old man might tell him. . . .

6

Fargo had stopped by the bank where Ken Ericson was vice president, but Ericson was in a meeting, so Skye had gone to visit Beth Conroy.

A Mexican woman answered Fargo's knock on the front door of the neat Queen Anne–style house. She was just past the point of first bloom but she would retain her appealing face into middle age. She wore a red blouse and a black skirt. Her English was very good.

"I was just going to shop for Miss Conroy," she explained. She didn't look terribly impressed with Fargo. Wary, yes, but not impressed in any positive way. Despite a shave and clean clothes, there was a sense of danger about him, like an animal that hadn't yet been domesticated. "Is there something I could help you with?"

"I need to talk to Miss Conroy." Fargo introduced himself and tapped a finger against his badge. "I'm a temporary deputy."

The woman smiled. "Senor, the Conroys are very important people. Badges do not intimidate them. One of those fine Victorian houses on the bluffs belongs to her father. When they moved in there they gave this house to Miss Conroy. That should tell you something about how much money they have."

"Is she here?"

"She's taking tea on the porch in back. She likes her privacy. She receives very few visitors. She also likes to be left alone. Especially since the Standish girl was killed. She wishes she'd been kinder to her."

"That's what I want to talk to her about. And I want you to go tell her that."

Fargo's tone was harsh. The conversation was over. He had now given her an order. Her first impulse was to refuse him. But now she knew that she had made her case and there was nothing else she could do but comply.

She turned and walked away. She'd made a point of not inviting him inside. While she was gone, he watched a gray tomcat who was in bad need of a diet evaluate him with deep green eyes. The tom didn't seem much impressed, either. This was a house of snobs, right down to the cat.

When the Mexican woman returned, she said, "Miss Conroy asks if you could come back tomorrow. She has a headache today and would like to lie down. She hopes you will understand."

"I don't understand," Fargo said. "Either I get her permission to come into the house or I just walk in and take care of any obstacles in my way if I need to."

For the first time the woman showed fear. "She's not used to violence. Violence upsets her greatly."

"Then tell her to see me now. No violence necessary if she'll just give me a few minutes to talk to her."

Behind the woman, a soft feminine voice said, "It's all right, Estella. I'll see this man. You go on about your shopping."

"Do you want to be alone here with him?"

"I'll be fine."

And then Fargo got his first glimpse of her. She was a rangy beauty, almost as tall as Fargo, a raven-haired, ivory-skinned, somewhat haughty young woman whose filmy yellow sundress did little to conceal the chic curves of her body. Her expression of amusement surprised him and he wondered what it was all about. The Mexican woman had found him frightening. This woman found him amusing. A strange household.

Beth Conroy said, "We're not used to having people like you in our house, are we, Estella?"

"I should say not. I'd watch out for him."

Beth had obviously taken note of how Fargo had assessed her body, especially her jutting breasts and round hips. "Oh, I think I can control him if I need to, Estella."

She said this without taking her eyes off Fargo's face. "Don't you think so, Mr. Fargo?"

"I'll go on then, miss."

"Don't hurry back. Take your time."

Estella's face wrinkled in confusion. Why would a proper young lady like Miss Conroy want to be left alone with a gunny like this Fargo man? Well, one thing she'd learned about working for rich people—they didn't hesitate to act on their whims.

After the front door closed, Beth said, "Are you as dangerous as you look?"

"Not unless I have to be."

"A lot of the locals think I'm dangerous, too."

He glanced around. From what he could tell the house was furnished in the style called French provincial. He'd seen pictures of this kind of decoration and furnishing in magazines. To him much of it looked spindly, but that was probably the beauty of it to wealthy people. A good deal of what they considered fashionable seemed eminently perishable to Fargo, as if it would barely last until the next fad came along.

"I'm having cold tea. Would you care for some, Mr. Fargo?"

"That'd be fine. But I want to get down to business because I've got a busy day ahead of me."

A coy glance. "Are you and the sheriff worried about a lynch mob tonight? Poor Jane was practically a saint to everybody around here. A man delivering things from the general store said that Donlon isn't expected to last through the night. There's going to be a real war if the sheriff won't hand Donlon over."

Fargo wished he didn't find her so sexually arousing because her arrogance irritated him. She sounded like a spoiled princess in a storybook castle. But this was Nevada and it was one hell of a long way from fantasyland.

He went out and sat on a screened-in porch. The grass sloped to the desert and was so thoroughly brown it could almost pass for desert itself. The furnishings here were more practical, a metal table and metal chairs, except for a divan, which was no doubt where the princess parked her ass.

33

She came out in a flurry of scents, perfume, sex and tobacco. Women had just begun to smoke in small numbers but they still had to hide it to avoid being heralded as sluts. Church people were very exacting moral judges.

"How's the tea?" she asked when she stretched out on the divan.

"Was Ken Ericson with you the night Jane Standish was murdered?"

"My, you *do* want to get down to business, don't you?"

"That isn't an answer."

"For God's sake, I'm not some sort of criminal. You could at least be polite."

"If he was with you, I need to know what time he met you and what time he left you."

"People think I'm happy she's dead. That isn't true."

Fargo shook his head. "People put up with you like this, do they?"

She laughed huskily. "The men want to sleep with me and the women want to kill me. How about you, Mr. Fargo? You're a man. At least I think you are. Do you want to sleep with me?" Then she narrowed her eyes and saw the anger in his gaze. "Oh, God. I just try to have a little fun on a sweltering day and you want to go and ruin it with your stupid questions." She took a dramatic sip of tea and said, "He came for dinner at seven and left around eleven o'clock."

"You're sure of that."

"Quite sure. That's part of our routine. Dinner here one night a week and then dinner at his place a different night of the week. A pretty exciting life, wouldn't you say?"

"You're willing to swear to that under oath?"

A hesitation of not more than two seconds but a hesitation nonetheless. "Of course."

He knew there wasn't any point pushing her. The hesitation told him she was lying but she wasn't likely to change her story.

"She broke off her engagement to him."

"That's right." The mocking tone was back. "And I picked up her discard."

"He had reason to hate her and so did you."

"Because he tried getting back with her while he was

34

engaged to me?" A smile that was more a leer than anything. "Don't think I didn't make him pay. He was a very lonely, frustrated man for three months after he embarrassed himself and me by chasing after her again."

No sex. This woman knew how to play the game, all right. Cut Ken Ericson off. One hell of a punishment for being bad.

"And he'll tell me the same thing? That you were together from seven till eleven?"

"Of course." Then her gaze filled with amusement again. "Are you thinking that we killed her together and worked up this alibi to protect ourselves? You have quite an imagination, Mr. Fargo."

He had many other calls to make before nightfall. No sense in wasting any more time here with the princess.

He stood up. "Thank you for the tea and your time."

She slithered off the divan. "I am a bitch, aren't I?"

He turned to pick up his hat and just as he was about to slide it on his head, he found her in front of him. She hooked an arm around his side and stepped closer to him. She kissed him without warning, her tongue spearing apart his lips, her hips moving hard against his.

She was a woman of surprises, a self-described bitch one moment, a comely seductress the next. She slipped from his embrace and dropped to her knees, skillfully undoing the buttons of his Levi's and taking his enormous shaft into her mouth without hesitation. Fargo had to smile. He'd been woman-bereft for a time but he sure was making up for it in this Nevada town.

She artfully began to drive him into ecstasy with a tongue that was downright magical. He felt his legs go weak from the pure pleasure she was giving him. And while her tongue was busy, she managed to strip him of his boots and jeans. She was one efficient woman.

But she had her own bliss in mind, too. Because just as she brought him to the point where he would spend himself, she pushed him back on the wide divan, ripped away her dress and then mounted him.

She rode him as she would a fine steed in a race. He sucked at her swaying breasts as she goaded both of them home, to the final joy that they would share together. Hot

juices flowed from her to cover Fargo's thighs. She began to bite at his neck, almost smothering him with her breasts. What a way to die, he thought playfully.

And then she slowed the pace and began moving up and down purposefully on him, her hips moving with such knowing ease that he gave himself over completely to the moment that was about to give both of them blinding elation.

And when it came, they thrashed about so violently that they slid off the divan and onto the floor of the screened-in porch.

Fargo laughed, even though he still didn't trust her. "I don't even care that you lied to me. Soon as I leave here I'll care. But right now—"

"Shut up, Fargo. That was just the first act."

And damned if it wasn't another twenty minutes before he managed to get out of there.

"You get out of here, Skunk! You know you can't come in here!"

Cyrus Corrigan spotted Skunk even before the ungodly creature had crossed the threshold of Corrigan's general store. Nobody would want to buy anything that had even been in the vicinity of Skunk.

Corrigan now came rushing around the penny-candy display he'd just filled up. If he had to hold Skunk back by force, then the wiry seventy-one-year-old would damned well do it.

Skunk was kept alive by Maude over to the café, who fed him out the back door twice a day. He slept wherever he could find shelter. One of the many Skunk jokes was that he'd slept in the livery one night and all the horses died from the stench.

To Corrigan, Skunk always looked like a man who'd just emerged from a raging fire. He was covered in a greasy black sheen, his hair a rat's nest of filth and vermin, his black stubs of teeth something you looked away from instantly—if you wanted to keep your most recent meal from coming back up on you.

And now this monstrosity wanted to walk among all of Corrigan's hard-earned treasures?

36

"You stay right there, Skunk!" Corrigan snapped, grabbing a broom and turning it around so that he could use the handle to keep Skunk not only at bay, but to push him back outside where he belonged.

Corrigan's nose wrinkled as he drew nearer. He said, almost in amazement, "What the hell you thinkin', Skunk? You know better than this, don't you?"

And then Skunk grinned. Not simply smiled. Grinned. "I'll be comin' in here real soon and spending a lot of money, Mr. Corrigan. And you'll have to treat me nice."

Now it was Corrigan's turn to grin. "You find your own line of silver, did you, Skunk?"

"You think I'm jokin', Mr. Corrigan, but I ain't. I'm comin' into some money and I'm gonna spend a lot of it right here in your store. I'm buyin' me a suit and a fancy cravat and I'm gonna eat over to the café—right inside with everybody else. Sit right by the front window there and watch the people go by. Just like normal folks do."

Odd, Corrigan thought. Skunk didn't usually come up with wild tales. Did he actually believe that he was coming into money? "Well," Corrigan said, "the first thing I'd do with that money is get yourself a bath and a shave." His voice was not unkind, even though he still held the broom handle near Skunk's chest like a sword. "Then you'll be ready for some new duds. But it won't do you any good to get new duds unless your body's clean. You follow me?"

"Oh, I follow you all right, Mr. Corrigan. I follow you real good."

And with that, Skunk began his retreat from the doorway of Corrigan's general store, leaving the owner to stand there, still perplexed by Skunk's story. Coming into money? Skunk? Now that was a whopper if Corrigan had ever heard one.

The time was just after noon. The heat was so sharp against the skin it reminded Fargo of being slashed with a knife. Pretty soon the skin would crack open just the way it would under the pressure of a sharp blade. That was how it felt, anyway.

Fargo was just reaching the business district when he saw

them approaching. A pair of them and he didn't have any doubt about their mission. They were gunnies in the hire of somebody. Fargo wondered who.

One was tall; one was short. One had long blond hair; one was bald. One was young; one was old. Both wore Colts in black leather holsters strapped to their waists.

The young one said, "I'll bet you're Fargo."

"Something I can do for you?"

Fargo saw how they were going to play it. The old man moved to the right. The young one would attack Fargo from the front; the old one would move around behind.

The only thing to do was attack first. Fargo took two steps forward, surprising the young one with a sharp left to the jaw and then a smashing right to the ribs. The young one clutched himself and dropped to his knees. Fargo figured he'd at least cracked if not broken a couple of those ribs.

The old one leapt on Fargo's back. What he hadn't figured on was Fargo anticipating this and bending down, so that while he touched Fargo's back momentarily, he kept right on going, flying over Fargo and landing right on top of his partner.

"It's too hot for this," Fargo said to the stunned gunnies. "Tell your boss that he should wait and send you out at night. It'll be cooler then and I'll be in a better mood to fight."

Then he eased his Colt from his holster and said, "Pitch those guns as far as you can. And do it right now."

The old one groused a few dirty words to himself. Unfortunately for him, he had his right hand flat against the dusty street trying to push himself to his feet.

Fargo stepped on his hand, putting all his weight into the effort. The old one cried out.

They didn't need any more persuading to toss their guns a good distance from where they sat in the street.

This was a necessary precaution. If they'd still had their guns, they just might have felt tempted to shoot the Trailsman in the back. You just could never be too cautious around gunnies.

7

"I just want you to know that I'd be willing to throw in with you tonight, Henry, but I've got this problem with my eyes. Don't think I could be all that much help."

Sheriff Henry Cawthorne nodded to his old church friend Clem Atkins. Clem was a hunting friend of his as well as a fellow member of the church choir. Both men had good voices even at their advanced ages. Clem was a small man with a nervous tic in his left eye and an unfortunate problem with his bowels that he rarely stopped talking about.

This was the third old friend who'd stopped by the sheriff's office to tell Cawthorne that they wouldn't be able to help. They weren't lying, of course, and their reluctance had nothing to do with cowardice. If a lynch mob materialized tonight they wouldn't, in fact, be much help. One couldn't see; one had lost an arm in the war; and one suffered from the inability to stay awake much past suppertime. Not exactly a trio that could hold off a mob.

Cawthorne was no stranger to sieges. He'd served five different towns as peace officer over the years, and inevitably—the West being what it was with circuit judges coming around only occasionally and hotheaded mobs coming around frequently—he'd faced crises pretty much alone.

People had to consider their standing in the community before they threw in with the law. If the majority of people wanted a lynching and you stood in their way, you just might find yourself ostracized. There was even the possibility that when the crowd rushed the jail to drag the prisoner out, some hothead just might "accidentally" kill you in the process.

Cawthorne understood the reasoning. But that didn't make him any more sympathetic. Towns were defined by how they honored their laws. It was pathetic that the only three who'd stopped by to express their regrets that they couldn't help were old men like himself. Young men should have been stopping by and offering not regrets but the force of their youth and the power of their guns. Did they want to raise their children in a town that was given to lynch law?

"Well, maybe I'll be lucky, Clem," Cawthorne said. "Maybe things'll settle down by tonight."

But he could see in his old friend's faded blue eyes that Clem didn't believe him. Hell, he didn't believe himself. Somebody was pushing this lynching idea. He was still wondering what Standish's men were doing off work and drinking it up in saloons.

"At least you got Rooney," Clem said, blowing his nose into a well-greened handkerchief.

"Yes," Cawthorne said ironically, "at least I've got Rooney."

And that was another possibility. Maybe Standish, who'd inflicted Rooney on Cawthorne, was behind the lynching. That would make sense. His beautiful and very sweet daughter had been stabbed to death. His wanting revenge— immediate revenge—would be only natural. And he had the power to make it come true. Standish got his way in this town.

"How's Bryce doin' back there?" Clem asked.

"Finally got to sleep. He raised holy hell for a couple of hours. Started to drive me crazy."

"You think he done it?"

"Looks that way. But looks don't always tell the truth. That's why we have trials. Try and get to the truth." He smiled at himself. "I sound as pompous as a politician, don't I?"

"You're a good man, Henry. I just wish I could help you tonight—or whenever you need me."

"Like I said, Clem, the people who should be helping me are the young ones. This is where they're going to raise their kids. They have more of a stake in this than we do.

40

But I'm afraid they aren't gonna do a damned thing about it. There'll probably be a fair number of them in the mob."

Cawthorne walked over to the barred window to the left of the front door. He could see the men who'd challenged Fargo standing in front of the Diamond Gal saloon, much drunker than they'd been earlier. They were waving at people, trying to draw them in so they could enlist them in this whole idea of razing the jail tonight and finding a nice sturdy branch that wouldn't crack when Bryce Donlon's neck snapped. But Standish hadn't counted on how unreliable they'd be. A few beers was one thing but these men were bobbing-and-weaving drunk. And the people they were trying to enlist just waved them off and kept going on their way. Who had time for men drunk at this time of day?

A small amusement but something anyway, Cawthorne thought. Maybe everybody who might be inclined to join the mob might get so soused they'd forget all about lynching. Maybe all they'd be able to do was puke and piss their brains out the way they did at the Fourth of July celebrations.

"Well, Henry, I need to be gettin' home to Ida. She always waits lunch for me. And she gets scared when I'm not there on time. Thinks at my age I'm just gonna keel over and die someplace." He touched the arm of his old friend. "I hate to leave you alone," he said.

Yeah, Cawthorne thought, *alone doesn't sound real good about now. Not good at all.*

Fargo had never given banks much consideration except for an idle thought about robbing one or two of them. That is, until he'd read a sarcastic piece in a newspaper about how banks were really churches for rich people who no longer believed in God. Their deity was money. And they weren't much inclined to share that money with poor people, either.

He'd sort of adopted that attitude as his own. And now, as he entered the bank where Ken Ericson worked, he was struck by how everybody spoke in such low voices, just the way they would in church. Except they were venerating cold, hard cash.

There were two teller windows amidst the fancy white-

and-gold wallpaper and the four desks where the bank officers faked smiles for the sake of all the lesser beings who approached them. The vault had been fixed in the right of the rear wall, and next to it were two offices where the president and the vice president respectively resided. Maybe they thought that their proximity to the vault would somehow intimidate anybody foolish enough to think of robbing the place.

A very kempt middle-aged woman wearing an enormous brooch just below her gathered lace collar took one look at Fargo and decided that here indeed was a lesser being. He resembled one of those scurvy creatures you always saw on the covers of yellowbacks, those trashy and highly unlikely tales that young boys and—for heaven's sake, some girls—read by the box load. She hoped that the security guard—an oldster named Hemingway—was watching this one, because he might very well be a robber. And that badge he wore couldn't possibly be real, could it? Maybe it was part of his robber's disguise.

"May I help you?" she said, her voice implying that she couldn't imagine a single thing she could do for the likes of him.

"I'd like to see Mr. Ericson."

"Mr. Ericson?" She sounded stunned.

"Yes. You've heard of him?"

His sarcasm stained her cheeks red.

"Of course I've heard of him," she snapped. "And I don't cotton to any mockery from you."

"The guard told me he was in his office. Mr. Ericson, I mean."

"The guard had no right to tell you that."

He felt a bit awkward about doing it but he tapped the badge that she had steadfastly refused to acknowledge. "He didn't have any choice. I'm Sheriff Cawthorne's new deputy, Skye Fargo." He smiled. "That probably makes you want to pick up and leave town, doesn't it?"

She harrumphed beneath her breath but stood up and without another word departed for Ken Ericson's office. Fargo was pretty sure he hadn't made a new friend.

While he waited for her return, Fargo noticed a woman at another, smaller desk taking note of him. She offered

him an impish smile that was unmistakably sexual. Surprising in a woman who looked so schoolteacher prim. Did they have to pass a primness test to work in this place? Fargo returned the smile. But then a male employee, swollen with self-importance, stepped over to her desk and imperiously tossed some papers down in front of her. Seemed like a decent sort of fellow if you liked stuffy blowhards.

A few minutes later, Fargo entered a small but well-appointed office with real mahogany wainscoting, an imposing mahogany desk and several framed nature drawings of eagles.

Ken Ericson was a slender man in a white shirt, a blue detailed cravat, blue suspenders and blue trousers. His blue suit coat hung on a coat tree in the corner. He was handsome enough but there was a sense of anxiety about him that spoiled his looks. He should have been a lot more self-confident. Even before the man spoke, Fargo wondered what he was so nervous about.

"I hope you don't mind that I'm not wearing my jacket," Ericson said. "It's pretty darn hot today."

"Sure is."

"Please. Have a seat." And then as he was seating himself, he said, "So you're Henry's new deputy."

"That's right."

"There's a lot of talk about you. Henry doesn't hire deputies very often."

Small talk. Fargo hated it. He said, "I'm just trying to figure out where everybody was the night Jane Standish was killed."

Ericson's eyes reflected surprise, suspicion. "That's odd."

"Why is that odd?"

"Well, this sounds like an investigation."

"That's what it is."

"But why? Everybody knows that Bryce Donlon killed her. And you've got Donlon in jail."

"Donlon says he's innocent."

Ericson laughed heartily—too heartily. "My God, man. Have you ever met a killer who didn't say he was innocent? Aside from a few gunnies who like to brag, I mean." This kind of cynicism coming from a pampered man in his early twenties seemed forced. What the hell did he know about

43

killers? Fargo wondered. But it was probably the right note to strike if you wanted to scoff at the idea that anybody but Donlon might have killed her.

"I just want to make sure that Donlon's the man. That's just what a good peace officer does, Mr. Ericson. You don't have anything against a peace officer just doing his job, do you?"

Ericson's cheeks colored. "No, of course not. That's a ridiculous thing to say." Again he was trying to bluster his way through an answer.

"Then you won't mind me asking a few questions?"

"Be my guest." But the right hand that lay flat on the desk twitched three times. And the anxiety was back in the blue eyes. He looked like an animal that knew it was about to be punished.

"I just need to know where you were that night."

Too quickly, Ericson said, "With my fiancée. Beth Conroy."

"I see. And where was this?"

"Her home. We eat together there once a week." Ericson leaned forward. "I would think that's all you need to know. I told you where I was and in this town my word is good. Damned good, in fact."

Fargo said, "Did you hate Jane Standish, Mr. Ericson?"

"Of course not. And I resent you saying anything like that."

"She chose not to marry you."

"That happens. Happens quite a lot, especially to young people."

"How did you handle it?"

Ericson glowered at him. "Henry's going to hear about this. And right now I'm damned tired of your questions."

"Just doing my job."

"Your job? Is it your job to come in here and pry into my past? No, I didn't handle it well, if you want to know. It took me several months to really get back on my feet. I'm embarrassed about how badly I dealt with it. I hated her and I loved her. You know how that is when a woman passes you over. But in the long run it was probably good for me. It made me grow up. I'd always had everything my own way. My father's a very powerful man in these parts.

He protected me from failing. But this was one thing he couldn't protect me from. So in that way Jane did me a favor. I had to face what happened alone. And now I can see that it was good for me."

A quiet knock. The door opened and the prim young woman leaned in and said, "I have those papers for you to sign. We need to get them on the stage in the next hour."

"Fine, Amy, bring them in."

Amy wore a yellow cotton dress that attempted in vain to disguise the fact that she was shapely beneath the material. Fargo particularly fancied the way the dress fell across her buttocks, emphasizing the rhythm of her hips as she crossed to the desk.

Ericson took the papers from her, then said, "In fact, Fargo, this woman walked me to Miss Conroy's that very same night. We'd both worked late here and since she lives in the same area as Beth, we walked there together." He glanced at Amy. "Isn't that right, Amy? I'm talking about the night Jane was killed."

"Oh, yes, of course. All those papers we had to file for the state capital." She glanced at Fargo, then back to her boss. "I need to get back to my desk, Mr. Ericson. I'll stop back for the papers."

"A very good employee," Ericson said when she'd left.

"Seems like it."

Ericson indicated the papers Amy had brought in. "I hope that's enough for you, Fargo. I'm very busy, as you can see."

Fargo knew he wasn't going to get any more information from this man. He hadn't gotten much useful, anyway. He stood up, picked up his hat and said, "Appreciate the time, Mr. Ericson."

"Sorry if I got a little irritable. Just all the work I have to do." He stood up, too, and came around the desk and shook hands with Fargo. It was a practiced handshake, one he made many times a day to a better class of customers. "One piece of advice, though, Mr. Fargo. Everybody knows that Donlon killed poor Jane. If you try to say otherwise, a lot of people are going to feel they might have to take the law into their own hands. And I don't think you want that, do you?"

"A man just might take that as a threat, Mr. Ericson."

"Just the facts of life, Mr. Fargo. Just the facts of life."

Tyler Rhodes knew what the knock on his den door meant. It would involve his son, Frank. Tyler was working at home today because he was afraid he might appear too distracted to his employees. He didn't want anyone to think that there was anything wrong in his life. It was important that everyone think that, as the second richest man in this area, right behind Standish, he had no particular worries.

Jenny, his wife of thirty years, walked into his office and said, "I had a terrible nightmare last night." Jenny was no longer the slender strawberry blonde he'd married, but even with the added weight her face was as sweet and pretty as it had been when he'd first started courting her. And his love for her was just as vital, too.

She seated herself in a leather chair, watched him as he placed his pen in the inkwell.

"I can't think of anything else," she said, touching her hand to the breast of her fine, white silk blouse.

"Neither can I."

"He was so drunk he doesn't remember coming here. So maybe he doesn't remember—"

"I keep trying to explain all that blood he had on his hands and shirt when he staggered in here."

"So do I. I pray over and over again that there's some other reason for the blood. That it didn't have anything to do with—"

"I just don't see how you could forget doing something like that. No matter how drunk you were."

Jenny sat silent for a time, watching grief playing on her husband's narrow but handsome face. "I wish he'd never started seeing her. He should've known how fickle she was." She paused. "But he'll learn to love somebody else."

"I think that's only in books. Learning to love somebody. Either you love them or you don't."

She was far too caring a person to tell him that in fact she'd learned to love him. She'd lost her true love to another woman and had been eager to escape the small town where she'd had to face humiliation every day. She'd met Tyler at a barn dance. He'd courted eagerly and briefly. They

were married after knowing each other less than ninety days. For three years she'd led a secret life of anger and longing. She wondered if she'd ever get over the man who'd deserted her. But a few years after giving birth to young Frank, she began to see what a good father Tyler was to the boy. And somehow in her admiration for the man, a kind of love began to emerge. Not the vital kind she'd felt for her true love but a slow, sure sense of *belonging* to him, as if he had earned her in some way. Not an ideal love, to be sure. But one she was comfortable with. And one that would endure even beyond the grave.

"He could hang," Tyler said.

"That's what my nightmare was about."

"Maybe we should send him away so that they could never find him."

"I don't know if I could stand that, Tyler. To never see our son again?"

He sighed. It was the weary sigh of an old man. But he wasn't old. He was just exhausted with this whole terrifying event. "There's only one thing that can help him."

"What's that?"

"There's talk of lynching Donlon tonight. I know Ted Standish wants it done. I heard some men talking when I walked to the post office." He glanced out the mullioned window at empty blue sky. "If they hang him, the matter'll be closed. I'm going to pay Ted a visit and see if there's any way I can help him."

"God, Tyler. I never thought I'd hear either of us talk like this. We're supposed to be decent people."

He looked at her with the harsh eye of the protector. "He's our son, Jenny. We don't have any choice."

8

Right now the feeling in the town was one of tension. Everybody above the age of seven was assuming that something terrible was going to happen tonight. Something terrible—and fun.

As much as Fargo didn't like to think this way, he knew that some folks enjoyed anything that took them out of their daily lives for even so much as a half hour. Something new and remarkable and memorable. And a lynching was perfectly fine for being new and remarkable and memorable.

Of course, they would pretend otherwise. They would say that as much as they didn't want to do it, they were only carrying out the unwritten law of bringing justice to a killer. They might even say, if something went wrong, the man not dying for a long, ugly time for example, that they'd tried to stop it. "Yessir, there I was begging these drunken fellas to stop and let the judge come around. But you know how it is with drunken fellas, don't ya?"

So right now the mood at two thirty p.m. was somber except in the saloons, where beery laughter never ceased.

But by tonight—the town would become a dark carnival of madmen and gawkers, and of powerful men having their own way despite the best efforts of the lawman here to keep things civilized.

Fargo was less than a half block away from the bank where he'd questioned Ken Ericson when a tall, thin man in a city suit approached him and said, "Mr. Standish would like me to talk with you. My name's Danning."

"I take it you work for him?"

"I run the office here. Mr. Standish and I go way back."

"I can probably save you a lot of time."

"Oh? And how's that?"

"Mr. Standish would like it if I left town before tonight and left the sheriffing to Cawthorne and Rooney."

Danning had a surprisingly sincere smile. "Well, you're half right. But you're making it sound like a threat. What Mr. Standish has in mind is more in the way of an opportunity."

Maybe it was because it was too hot to stop and see what was going on. But nobody seemed to pay any attention to the two men standing well into the street. Women with parasols and men with derbies hurried by on the board sidewalks and buggies and wagons pressed on without drivers or passengers even glancing in their direction.

Danning reached inside the dark suit jacket he wore and pulled forth a long white envelope. He held it up for Fargo to see. He seemed very proud of this envelope, as if it might hold the secret to nothing less than immortality, or at least how to beat hangovers in the morning. "For a man like yourself, this is a true opportunity."

"I'll bet."

"Don't scoff, Mr. Fargo. There's four thousand dollars in here. Good Yankee money. Enough for a man to buy himself a nice farm and some good livestock and settle down for life."

"Or head to San Francisco and have a whole lot of fun on the Barbary Coast."

"To me that would be a very foolish waste of an opportunity but it would be your money and your call."

"Afraid I'm not interested."

Beneath the rim of his wide-brimmed hat Danning's green eyes expressed true surprise. "You're not interested in four thousand dollars?"

"Guess not."

"Have you ever even *seen* four thousand dollars?"

"Sure. Several times. None of it was mine. But I saw it, anyway."

"You realize that things could get dangerous tonight. Mr. Standish is in no way encouraging that."

"Of course not."

49

"Even though it was his own daughter who was murdered by Donlon, Mr. Standish is willing to wait for the judge to come to town for a fair trial to be held."

"He's one hell of a gent, Mr. Standish is. I'm sorry about his daughter. From everything I've heard she was a very nice young woman. But that doesn't give him the right to try bribing somebody."

"It's not a bribe. It's a business opportunity. I've told you that."

"I'm afraid I still can't do it, Mr. Danning. Cawthorne's a good man but he's getting old fast. He needs help. You know and I know—and so does Mr. Standish, who you say has nothing to do with it—that there's going to be a lynching tonight. Or a damned good try at one, anyway. Cawthorne'll lay down his life before he'll let that happen."

"He has Rooney."

"And Rooney does exactly what Mr. Standish tells him." Danning's lips pursed in great displeasure. "What is it you're suggesting?"

"I'm not suggesting anything. Not right now. Because I don't have the facts to back it up. But I find it strange that Mr. Standish—who doesn't want a lynching to take place—is willing to pay me a hell of a lot of money to leave town so I can't help Cawthorne."

"He'll be very disappointed when I tell him this."

"Well, tell him that I'm sorry about his daughter, which I am. But that I'm not convinced that Donlon killed her."

This time the green eyes expressed shock. Genuine shock. "Don't be ridiculous. Everybody knows he killed her. Three people saw him running away from the scene."

"That part's true from what I can gather. But did you ever think that maybe she was already dead when he found her?"

The lips pursed again. The green eyes burned with dissatisfaction. "You'll still have some time to reconsider, Mr. Fargo. I hope for your sake—and the sake of the town—that you'll do that."

He nodded, turned and walked away, a slightly hunched man who moved with the ease of a shadow.

* * *

When Clyde Rooney saw the boy on the street, his stomach twisted and his face got even hotter than the scorching heat could make it. He stepped quickly into the telegraph office so the boy wouldn't see him.

Mark Jackson was now ten years old. Rooney was well aware of this. Too well aware of his age. People said he was the smartest boy in the little school all the kids went to. They also said that they saw big things for him in the future. As far as Rooney knew, nobody had ever said anything like this about any of the town's children, including those of the Standishes or the Rhodeses.

Rooney stood at the window of the telegraph office, noting the progress of the blond-haired boy as he made his way up the street, book in one hand and a baseball glove in the other. That was the other thing. Not only was Mark brilliant, he was also a hell of a good athlete. The fastest kid in races, the best pitcher the town had ever seen.

"Now there's a kid you could be proud of," Mr. Thompson, the telegrapher, said. "Not like some of those snots runnin' around and causin' trouble all the time." He spoke over the clatter of his machine. It was comforting to know that important words could come from virtually anywhere in the world and eventually reach you by telegraph. The clatter of the machine was therefore pleasing to Mr. Thompson, who considered himself to have the most modern of all jobs in this little burg. For him the clatter was music, pure music.

"His dad comes in here sometimes," Mr. Thompson said. "And he's always braggin' on him. Anybody else, I'd be irritated. You know how folks are when they start braggin' on their children. But Don Jackson's actually got a kid *worth* braggin' about." He smiled. "And if my wife had a body like that wife of his—I'd be braggin' on that, too. What's her name again?"

Sarah, Rooney thought. *You stupid bastard, her name is Sarah.*

The name Rooney tried never to think of.

"Her name's Sarah."

"Say," Mr. Thompson said, "didn't you—"

"That was a long time ago," Rooney snapped.

"Well, sure, Rooney. I just meant that you and her—"

"That was when I met Helen. I decided she was better for me."

If Mr. Thompson was good at hiding disappointment, he was having an off day. Helen Cartwright, huh? She was a sweet woman and all that but she'd come from dirt and as for looks— Must be true love, Mr. Thompson thought to himself philosophically. Personally, how a man could walk away from Sarah's breasts and tempestuous face—well, there were a whole lot of songs about true love and true romance and only one girl in the world for me and—Mr. Thompson sure never would've married his Nora if she hadn't been sufficient up top. But then, maybe Rooney saw something in poor drab Helen that nobody else did—

He got the distinct impression that he'd irritated Rooney in some way. And that certainly hadn't been his purpose. He changed the subject. "Sounds like you'll have your hands full tonight, Rooney. A lot of talk about stringing up that Donlon boy."

"Lot of talk about a lot of things," Rooney snapped. "You just stick to your telegraph and don't worry about anything else."

Mr. Thompson first looked surprised and then looked angry. Being a deputy was one thing but being a trained telegrapher was another. Which of them had the most exciting job? Which of them had people stopping in all the time just to watch him work? "I was just tryin' to say that I hope things go all right for you. Next time I won't bother to be polite. How's that?"

Rooney sighed, frowned. "Sorry there, Thompson. Just have a lot on my mind."

Mr. Thompson felt a little better. Didn't pay to argue with the law. But then it didn't pay to take abuse when you didn't have it comin', either. He returned to what he believed was a safer subject. "You know, it sure would make a man proud to have fathered a boy like that Mark Jackson, wouldn't it?"

"Yeah," Rooney said, scanning the street. But the boy had disappeared. Probably turned left at the end of the block, left being where the baseball field was located. Play-

ing in this kind of heat was something only a fool would do. A fool or a kid.

"Yeah," he said again. "It sure would make a man proud to know he was the real father of a kid like that."

Not until Rooney had been gone for five minutes, did the word "real" come back to Mr. Thompson. He wondered why Rooney had used it. The "real" father. Didn't make a lot of sense.

Mr. Thompson shrugged and went back to his telegraph machine. Well, Rooney was probably so nervous about tonight he'd just misspoke.

Yes, that was probably it. He'd just misspoken.

9

Dottie Swinnerton was still dealing with the look and stench of the man named Skunk when the door to Frank Rhodes's law office opened up and in came another disreputable-looking cuss. True, this one didn't smell. And true, the blue eyes reflected both intelligence and a sense of propriety—this was a law office, after all, and one expected decorum, didn't one?—but still he had the look of a gunman about him. Not even his handsome face, which Dottie might have found reassuring otherwise, could disguise the air of menace the man brought with him. She pushed her nameplate forward as if it could shield her from harm.

"Afternoon, ma'am," he said politely enough. "My name's Skye Fargo." He properly removed his trail-worn hat. "I'm Sheriff Cawthorne's new deputy. I'd like to speak with Mr. Rhodes."

Well, Dottie thought, at least he has manners and knows all the right words. She couldn't fault him for being impolite, that was for sure. Still and all, she could easily imagine him snapping his gun free and dropping an opponent without mercy.

"And your business would be?"

"My business would be none of *your* business."

Well, there you had it. His true colors. Remarkable that he'd waited this long to be insulting. Just like Henry Cawthorne to hire some smart mouth like this. Somebody who'd say all the nasty things Henry himself was afraid to say.

"I don't appreciate sarcasm."

"Well, I don't appreciate being asked about private matters. I'm here on official business, Miss Swinnerton. If Mr.

54

Rhodes wants to tell you what we talked about afterward, that's fine with me. But for right now I need to talk to him in private."

"You could have said that in the first place," she said.

"Then you wouldn't have had to insult me."

Here was his perfect opportunity to apologize but she noticed that that didn't seem to be on his mind. Instead, he stared at the office with FRANKLIN RHODES scrolled in gold leaf on the door.

She stood up. "He may be too busy to see you."

"Unless he's having surgery in there, he'll see me now. I don't have a lot of time."

Her church group often commented to Dottie that she was too quick to judge others. In this case she could point out that her first impression was exactly right. Despite his pretense to good breeding, this man was a heathen and a blackguard. *Unless he's having surgery in there.* She supposed he thought himself very funny. Probably provided hours of amusement for the dim-minded men in the saloon.

She went to the door, knocked discreetly once and responded to "Yes?" by opening the door and peeking in. "There's a man to see you." Dottie made a horrific face so her boss would know what he was in for. "He says he's Henry Cawthorne's new deputy."

"'He says'? Does he have a badge?"

"He does."

Frank Rhodes hesitated. Dottie noted that her employer had suddenly taken on the appearance of someone stricken with terrible anxiety. He seemed to cower there in his chair. Why would he be afraid of seeing a deputy sheriff? This Fargo was no match for the breeding, education and wiles of a professional man such as Mr. Rhodes. If anything, it should be Fargo who was afraid of seeing Mr. Rhodes.

"Tell him to come by later. Tell him I'm busy right now."

With that, she stepped inside Rhodes's office and closed the door. She'd been speaking softly so Fargo couldn't hear her. But now she wanted to really tell her boss everything.

"I told him you might be busy and do you know what he said?"

"What?" Rhodes looked afraid to hear.

"He said, and I quote, 'Unless he's having surgery in there, he'll see me now.' "

Frank Rhodes gulped. His face was sheened with sweat. She suspected it wasn't only the merciless heat of the day that had caused the beads of perspiration to form across his forehead.

"He's very uncouth, Mr. Rhodes. Very uncouth. It's just like Henry to hire somebody like him."

She had just finished speaking when the door was pushed inward and she sensed somebody now standing behind her. "Afternoon, Mr. Rhodes," Fargo said. "I'm real happy you agreed to see me."

Henry Cawthorne was a drinker of green tea. He enjoyed beer sometimes and even whiskey on occasion. But for the most part he drank green tea. He believed it helped his bowels and his digestion and his eyesight. He realized that the last claim was dubious but no matter what those scientists had to say, Cawthorne felt he saw better for the first hour after taking one of four cups of tea a day.

Right now he wished he wasn't seeing so well. Right now Clyde Rooney, his deputy, walked in the front door of the sheriff's office with a mighty imposing rifle.

"You shooting some buffalo, are you, Clyde?"

"Just thought this might come in handy. For tonight."

The rifle he toted was a big fifty-caliber Sharps. Cawthorne had seen plenty of them in the Plains states. The way the dime novelists told it, one shot of a hundred and twenty grains of powder and the buffalo fell over dead. But Cawthorne knew better. A single shot would wound and sicken the animal but it would rarely kill him. Cawthorne had heard of men who'd had to put as many as ten shots into a buffalo before it was dead.

But one shot from a Sharps like this into a man . . . a completely different story.

"There're gonna be a whole lot of people disappointed tonight when nothing happens." Cawthorne laughed. "I know your boss Standish is trying to stir up trouble. And I have to say that maybe I'd do the same thing if it'd been my own daughter who'd been murdered. But I think most

people in our little town have sense enough to let the law take its course and leave well enough alone. And if a dozen or so drunks show up from the saloons, I'd say myself and Fargo can handle them without much trouble."

"What about me? I plan to help."

Amusement lighted Cawthorne's eyes. "You plan to do whatever Standish *tells* you to do. And right now I can't see Standish doing anything except making trouble." He nodded to the Sharps. "Fargo's got a Henry. That's a hell of a rifle, too."

"Yeah. But I wonder how good he is with it. I hunted buffalo. I wonder if he did."

Cawthorne said, "You and two other no-goods went to the Dakotas on a lark. You stayed there six days and then headed for the nearest whorehouse you could find. In my book that don't make you an expert. And it don't trick me into thinking that you're gonna be on my side tonight."

Rooney sat on the edge of the desk. "Now what the hell does that mean?"

"It means that you brought that Sharps in here so I'd think that you'd found the Lord and were actually going to do what I wanted you to do—instead of what Standish wanted you to do. But it won't wash. I don't want you here tonight. I don't trust you."

"You just got done saying that you didn't think anything was going to happen tonight."

"That's right. But in case it does happen, I need somebody I can trust. And that ain't you."

"I been a pretty good deputy." Rooney actually sounded hurt. Cawthorne almost laughed. "And anyway, Mr. Standish wants me here tonight. He said you'd probably try and keep me away. But he said to tell you he won't stand for it. He wants me here to make sure you don't try and sneak Donlon out of here."

"Orders from on high, huh?"

"Mr. Standish is a good man."

"You know, a lot of the time I'd agree with that. But right now he can't think straight. His daughter's dead and he wants vengeance. I don't always agree with his judgments but he never does anything that would hurt the town.

It's pretty much *his* town. But he's being reckless now. Real reckless. And I want to help him from doin' anything he'll regret."

"That's real nice of you, Sheriff," Rooney said. He made his sarcasm clear. He went to the door. "You'll be hearin' from him, I can guarantee you that. I'm gonna be here tonight one way or the other."

Cawthorne's wrinkled face cracked in a smile. "If you're tryin' to scare me, Rooney, you're doin' a piss-poor job. You know that?"

Rooney left.

At ten minutes to three, Skye Fargo stood in the exact spot where the body of young Jane Standish had been found.

He had come here directly from his meeting with Frank Rhodes. His useless meeting. Rhodes had proved to be so nervous that he'd spilled his coffee and nearly tripped when he stood up to escort Fargo from his office. But he had offered no real information about his whereabouts other than to say he'd spent most of the evening working, an alibi that Fargo found suspicious. He'd wanted to ask Rhodes many more questions but Rhodes's secretary insisted that Rhodes had a board of directors meeting he had to attend in the conference room. Fargo had the sense that the secretary had contrived the meeting to help out her boss. But he hadn't had much choice but to go along with what was likely a charade.

In daylight, the alley was anything but impressive. Road apples showed that this was a route used by wagons leaving the blacksmith's a block away. The large number of cats and kittens demonstrated their fealty to the back door of a café that put out milk for them and scraps of meat for dogs. There was a loading dock that a hobo could use to sleep on at night and from the looks of one corner of it, that was just what at least one hobo was doing. A small pile of cigarette butts and broken stick matches indicated that the guest sure enjoyed his smoking.

Fargo walked up and down the alley, accompanied by a black-and-white cat with a vivid pink nose. She had the starved, sweet look of the runt about her. She also had the eager look of an animal that devoutly hoped to be adopted.

The witnesses who claimed to have seen Bryce Donlon run from the alley could well be mistaken. Fargo wanted to make sure that their view was as unobstructed as they'd insisted it was. According to Cawthorne, who'd given him all this information earlier, the two women and the man were leaving town in a buggy after a late church supper. As their vehicle approached the alley, they said they saw Donlon appear suddenly, gape frantically in both directions and then lurch into a broken run toward a wooded area behind the false fronts on the other side of the street.

Donlon admitted finding her. Donlon admitted running from the scene. Donlon admitted being in love with her and bitter about it.

All very good reasons for Donlon to be the prime suspect.

The scrap of paper was wedged between a small piece of rock and the edge of a wooden step. Probably meant nothing but Fargo bent and snatched it up, anyway. Wasn't much to it, just the word "tonight" written in very tight, proper penmanship in a color of ink that was a brown of some kind. The significance of "tonight" came to him quickly. Who had lured Jane into the alley? Had somebody done so with this note? Most likely. He folded the scrap and tucked it into the pocket of his work shirt.

Fargo glanced down at the tiny black-and-white cat. If only she had some answers. She might very well have been here when Jane Standish was murdered.

He turned around and started back down the alley. The cat bounced on ahead of him, her tail twitching with great importance. The alley stank, the sun searing the rotting garbage from the café. The cat stopped and took a sharp right, walking beneath a parked wagon to a small barn. Fargo didn't pay much attention at first. He kept on walking, scanning right to left, left to right, for anything that might prove interesting. He was willing to accept that Donlon had killed Jane Standish. He just wanted to make sure that a serious effort had been made to prove it.

The cat now stood in the open barn meowing in his direction. She managed to sound both alarmed and pitiful. She probably hadn't had any milk in some time. He decided to go over and pick her up. But the cat wasn't interested in

making friends. It was obvious she was on some kind of inscrutable mission.

He went into the barn. The shadowy place was more of a storage facility than an actual barn. Several different kinds of wagons—everything from freight wagons to a Conestoga—various large farm implements, saddles, even stacks of lumber among many other items filled the place.

The cat stopped in front of a wagon. She went into her urgent meowing again. This was some cat. Part dog, if Fargo wasn't mistaken.

The wagon the cat seemed troubled by was a freight wagon, and the closer Fargo got to it the better he understood the feline's fascination with it. The smell. The barn was crowded with aromas—leather, wood, metal, oil, dirt floor, hay—but whatever was in the bed of the freight wagon superseded all other smells.

Fargo's face twisted in displeasure. Something rotten—something even more rotten than garbage left to fester in the sunlight—something damned near unholy. He couldn't imagine what could create this kind of odor.

And then it suddenly sat up and gawked at him. Fargo thought of the creature as an "it" rather than a "he" because his first impression was that nothing human could be this filthy. Hard to judge if the shabby clothes were dirtier than the pieces of exposed flesh. Hard to judge which was more offensive, the tiny blackened stubs of teeth or the pus-filled infections around the dark, inhuman eyes. Hard to judge which of the mixture of odors was most vile—the stench of vomit, liquor or flesh that had been allowed to crack and crawl with vermin of many kinds.

The man sitting on his knees reached into the left pocket of his soiled suit coat with a grubby hand and extracted a wedge of cheese the size of a silver dollar. He put it to his mouth and ripped a tiny piece free with the stubs of his teeth. He then spat what lay on his lip down to the cat below the wagon.

The cat began eating immediately.

Fargo had to smile about that. So the cat wasn't a dog, after all. Fargo had thought that the feline had been leading him to some kind of important clue. Fargo decided he'd read one too many magazine stories about clever dogs. All

this cat had wanted was food. And she obviously didn't give much of a damn if Fargo had followed along or not.

Now Fargo stared at the creature in front of him. The man was just now swinging his body over the side of the wagon and dropping to the earthen floor.

The stench bore such force that Fargo had to step back when the man turned around to face him. He smiled and it was a gesture both sad and savage. You had to pity such a creature as this—God alone knew what kind of life story a man like this had—but you had to be wary of him, too. He might be insane and thus capable of anything.

"They call me Skunk."

Fargo nodded.

"You afraid of me?"

"Nope."

"Most people hereabouts are."

But Fargo was thinking past the man's wretched looks and wondering if this barn was his usual resting place. If it was—or if his resting place was anywhere else in this alley—then he could be worth talking to.

"My name's Fargo."

"You got yerself one of them stars."

"The badge?"

"Yessir, the badge." He bowed his head, his dark hair a tumbled rat's nest that was pocked here and there with pieces of twig and assorted other bits of refuse.

"I'm Sheriff Cawthorne's deputy."

"He ain't as mean to me as some others."

"He seems like a good man."

"He even stops some of them from bein' mean to me. Sometimes they get drunk and they beat me up pretty bad."

No surprise there, Fargo thought. Every little town has at least one outcast. And it was always open season on them. So many lies were told about them that they became the stuff of myths, especially to children. They became inhuman in the eyes of the town and therefore it was all right to inflict any kind of violence on them. Fargo had heard of people like Skunk being set on fire and left to die in the flames.

"You know about Jane Standish being murdered?"

"Yessir."

"She was murdered in this alley right out here."

"Yessir."

"Is this where you usually sleep, in the barn here?"

"Most of the time."

"Were you sleeping in here the night she died?"

"Yessir. I suppose so, anyway."

"You don't know for sure?"

"Sometimes Skunk gets hisself confused sorta like."

"So you don't remember?"

Fargo had watched Skunk's eyes carefully as the man responded to his questions. The more they talked about Jane Standish's death, the more evasive the eyes became. Skunk began glancing away instead of looking directly at Fargo. Skunk was lying. Fargo didn't know *what* he was lying about, only that he had suddenly decided not to answer truthfully.

"I remember the commotion afterward, I guess. Sheriff Cawthorne and all them others bein' here and then her folks comin' down and all the cryin' and all the—commotion—like I said."

"Did you hear her cry out for help?"

"No, sir, I did not."

"Did you hear anybody talking to her?"

"No, sir, I did not." Glancing away frequently as he responded to the questions.

"So you must have been asleep, then."

"Yessir, I musta been."

"And the only thing that woke you up was the commotion afterward?"

"Yessir."

"And you were in here?"

"Yessir. In this very same wagon."

"You're lying."

Those two words drew Skunk up short. He reacted the way he would have to a hard punch to his solar plexus. It was as if all his wind—hell, all his life force—had suddenly, instantly been drained out of him.

Skunk dropped his gaze to the cat, who was nibbling on the last pieces of cheese. He opened his mouth to speak and—

The sound of gunshots emerged.

Fargo knew instantly that the gunfire had come from the street at the end of the alley. Main Street. He had many other questions for Skunk now that he was sure the man was lying but he also had no choice but to find out what was going on with the gunshots—especially since the shots kept coming.

He yanked his Colt from its holster and ran from the barn. If he'd had time he'd have found a length of rope and bound Skunk's wrists and ankles. But there wasn't even time for that.

You never knew what a drunk was going to do for the simple reason that the drunk himself didn't know what he was going to do.

And when you had a group of drunks things got much worse.

A group of six men, if you cared to call them that, had set up an archery target in the middle of Main Street. They were taking target practice with their handguns. To them, this was great good fun. Boys will be boys.

But it wasn't fun for the timid merchants who cowered on the sidewalk watching their customers—especially those with kids—vamoose from the business district. It also wasn't fun for the saloon keepers who'd lost all their drinkers to the dusty street. Who could miss out on watching a bunch of drunks shoot at an archery target—and miss. And Lordy did they miss. They shot out windows and they shot a few carriages and surreys and wagons. And they damn near shot the minister who was just coming back from visiting a very sick woman.

A fine old time was had by all.

Right up until the time Fargo arrived.

After wondering why Cawthorne hadn't already put a stop to this, Fargo decided to waste no time trying to reason with these men. Alcohol had made any serious discussion impossible.

The first man he walked up to, he coldcocked without warning. A straight right hand to the jaw. The man crumpled and eventually fell flat on his face.

The second man he encountered saw him coming and

went into a gunny crouch. Just as he was drawing his gun, Fargo smashed him in the forehead and when the man jerked upward, Fargo kicked him in the groin. He then grabbed the man's gun and tossed it far down the street.

The third man was so engrossed in watching the other three men sizing up the target that he didn't hear Fargo come up from behind until it was too late. Fargo got him around the throat and hit him with such force on the side of the head that the man was unconscious before Fargo flung him to the ground.

By this time the remaining men had not only become aware of Fargo, they had turned their beery attention to him. But one look at the three bodies of their friends cooled their initial impulse to take Fargo on.

This was particularly wise on their part because Fargo had his gun drawn while theirs were still in their holsters.

"Throw your guns down now or I start executing you one by one. And I'll start with you, Bowersox."

Bowersox was the bald man who'd led the thugs who'd confronted Fargo outside the sheriff's office earlier today. He'd fancied himself up somewhat since then. A dandy red kerchief was tied festively around his neck. For a man of such mean countenance the red kerchief looked awfully damned Eastern.

"Them men better be alive."

"One of them's groaning," Fargo said. "That's a pretty good sign he's still kicking."

"You're so damned smart. This ain't even your town. You don't know what goes on here."

"Same thing that goes on in every town, Bowersox. The lawman tries to do a good job and a bunch of drunken troublemakers try to stop him."

"If Cawthorne's so good, where is he now?"

Fargo tried to dismiss the remark by saying, "He's busy just the way I am. Now drop the gun."

As he watched Bowersox make a show of deciding what to do, Fargo thought about running him in. The problem was if Bowersox was in jail, there would be an added incentive for his friends to gather tonight. Fargo knew that Cawthorne—and he agreed with this—would give as few people as possible an excuse to be out on the street tonight.

"Time's up, Bowersox." Fargo raised his gun and pointed it directly at Bowersox's chest. Bowersox sneered. But he dropped his Colt. The other two complied immediately.

The merchants began drifting down off the sidewalk to fan out around Fargo. Their new protector.

"You know how much you drunkards cost us in business?" barked one of them.

"We should come up with an estimate and make every one of you share the cost," snapped another.

"If I had my way, I'd ask Mr. Fargo here to run every one of you out of town," cracked a third.

Fargo's eyes scanned the merchants. One of them held a six-shooter. "You keep your gun trained on them. A couple of you go and pick up their guns. Then you can supervise while they haul off the target and clean up the mess they made here in the street. After that, let them go. If any of them gives you any trouble, you have my permission to kill him on the spot." He grinned at Bowersox. "These merchants'd really enjoy getting rid of you boys, so I wouldn't give them any excuse."

"You're not the sheriff."

"Nope. I'm not. But I'm sure Cawthorne'll back me up on this."

"But that'd be cold-blooded murder," said one of Bowersox's punks.

"Well, let's see what a jury says." Fargo smiled. "I'll have one of the merchants here kill one of you and then we'll take it to trial and see what the verdict is." He looked over the sorry lot. "So I'll need a volunteer. Which one of you should the merchants kill?"

The merchants were laughing openly. It was their turn to have some fun.

Fargo said, "A couple of you men go pick up their guns and use them on those drunks if you have to till everything here is cleaned up. I've got other things I need to do."

"We appreciate this, Fargo," one of the merchants said. "Sure glad Henry hired you. Sure hope you can stay on."

Fargo nodded good-bye and then went off to see if the man named Skunk was still anywhere around the barn. It was a good bet he wasn't.

10

If anybody had tried this in his younger days, Henry Cawthorne would have seized the man's wrist and snapped it in half. In fact he'd done that very thing many times in his history of sheriffing in towns across the West.

But his younger days were long gone and this particular man—Bryce Donlon—knew that there was a good possibility that tonight he'd be lynched. So he didn't have much trouble at all snatching Cawthorne's gun from its holster.

There had been nothing brilliant about the way he'd hoodwinked Cawthorne into the cell. He'd pretended to be sick. Ever since he was a boy he'd been able to vomit pretty much on command. It was a good trick for ten-year-olds. People much past that age found it revolting. Who wanted to watch somebody puke?

But for once the trick had a practical application. When Henry heard him puking and then wailing, he hurried as fast as his arthritic legs would carry him and came back to the cells. He was already thinking he'd probably have to have the doc come in and take a look at Donlon. Maybe the kid had picked up some kind of bug in the desert. Desert illnesses could be a whole lot of trouble to deal with.

Unlocked the cell. Stepped inside. Saw the corner where the kid was kneeling next to the mess he'd made. Stepped over there. Made a face as the stench of vomit filled his nostrils. And then put a hand on Donlon's shoulder to see if he was all right.

And that was when it had happened. Donlon sprang up,

reached out and ripped Cawthorne's gun from its holster and then stuck the barrel of the gun into Cawthorne's side.

Cawthorne didn't know who to hate most—himself for being so stupid or Donlon for being just about the dumbest young man in the territory.

"I'm going out the back way."

"They'll find you and kill you, Bryce."

"This time I won't head for the desert."

"Wherever you go, they'll find you and bring you back."

"There a horse back there?"

"Mine."

"It's mine now."

"You're safer in here. Trust me."

Donlon grimaced. "You I trust, Sheriff. It's them I'm afraid of. They're ready to hang me no matter what. They don't even give a damn that I didn't kill her. They're not about to listen to me, either. So the way I see it, I don't have much choice."

"You're gonna break your sister's heart."

"She'll understand. Maybe not at first. But down the line. She'll know that what I did was right."

Cawthorne looked him over. Donlon didn't have any real appreciation for what he was up against. There would be a posse unlike this town had ever seen. And every single man in it would want the honor—the privilege—of killing Donlon. And that man would be a hero when he came back here. Standish would see to it. So would the newspaper editor. Probably some of the Eastern papers would pick up the story, too. It would be portrayed as this sadistic madman up against a good and honorable man. Even if Donlon got shot in the back, the story would go that there'd been a face-off and that against great odds this ordinary, common, everyday man had found the courage and pluck to take on this mad-dog killer and make the world right again.

But Donlon here was too scared and too callow to see any of this in his future. All he could think of was running.

"You say you're innocent."

Donlon snorted. "Save your breath, Sheriff. I don't *say* I'm innocent. I *am* innocent. But I don't have time for your

little speech about how the law will prove me right if I just give it time. I'll be swingin' from a tree by then and you know it." He stepped toward the cell door. "Now go over there and sit down on the cot."

Shaking his head, the lawman did as he was told. He wished somebody would come in about now and stop this fool kid from signing his own death warrant. Standish would get his way, after all. And unlike a lynching, death by posse was perfectly legal. Wouldn't be worth a legal challenge even if Donlon was shot unarmed. That situation could easily be faked—toss a six-shooter down next to Donlon's hand and say that it belonged to him. Not a thing the law could—or would—do about it.

But Cawthorne had been around too long to know that moments like these didn't have gallant men on white steeds riding to the rescue at the last minute. That was storybook stuff. No, Donlon would escape and would ride hard out of town. Cawthorne would be found sitting in the cell and Rooney would put together a posse. And they would divide up into three groups, each chasing a different direction. And no matter how long it took, no matter how rough the terrain got, no matter what the weather was like, they would hunt Donlon down and kill him.

No doubt Standish would be offering a big reward. The shooter would thus be not only a hero to the town, he would be a *rich* hero. And every time he told his tale of killing the notorious Bryce Donlon, the tale would get wilder, wild enough that the town's little kids would take to following him around like one of the heroes in the dime novels everybody read even if they said they didn't.

And Donlon would be long dead. And even if he was innocent, as he claimed, nobody would bother to look into Jane's death anymore because as far as the town was concerned, Donlon had killed her.

"I'm going to say it one more time, Donlon."

"I told you to save your breath." Donlon had taken Cawthorne's keys and was now locking the cell door. "I'll leave the keys on the front desk."

Cawthorne slumped against the wall, his bottom adjusting to the cot. He listened as he heard Donlon rushing

around in the office. He'd be grabbing saddlebags and stuffing them with any kind of food he could find. He'd also be taking a rifle and extra ammunition. Then he'd go slamming out to the back where Cawthorne's horse was ground-tied beneath a huge oak shade tree. Then he'd ride like hell out of town.

Cawthorne gave him a few minutes before he started yelling. Wouldn't be long before somebody heard him and came in to see what was going on.

Wouldn't be long before the posse was chasing after Donlon, who would've had, at most, a half hour head start.

On the way back to the sheriff's office, Fargo saw banker Ken Ericson's secretary walking toward him. She hadn't recognized him because her head was down. She was walking quickly, nervously, in the blistering sunlight. She was a shapely, appealing woman whose looks were spoiled somewhat by her state of perpetual agitation. She'd seemed anxious in Ericson's office when she'd agreed with her boss that she had, in fact, walked him to Beth Conroy's house the night of the murder. Fargo had put her anxiety down to the situation. But free of the bank and free of her boss, she still gave an impression of apprehension.

Even when she nearly bumped into Fargo, she didn't look up. He had to take her elbow to get her attention. She raised her head, her pert face registering surprise. "Oh, Deputy Fargo, I should watch where I'm going." She smiled distractedly.

People came and went around them. Nearby, a group of five children played some kind of shoot-out game. This entailed running in the heat. A generation of lunatics, Fargo thought and almost laughed. But then every generation of kids could be accused of that. And the cynical might say that they only got crazier as they got older.

Amy started to walk around him, heading fretfully on her way. But his voice stopped her. "That was good of you to help your boss out."

"Oh?" She was unsure of what he meant.

"When you said you'd walked with him to Beth Conroy's the other night."

"Oh." She wasn't much of a liar. Her cheeks filled with blood and her gray eyes were uneasy. "I—I just told the truth was all, Deputy Fargo."

"Well, I'm just checking up on everybody's whereabouts and it's always helpful when somebody can back up somebody else's claim."

She'd started nibbling on her lower lip. "And anyway, isn't Bryce Donlon the one under arrest?"

"Yes, he is. But he claims he's innocent. Be terrible to see a man hanged based on lies, wouldn't you say?"

The worry in her lovely eyes increased. "Yes. Yes, it would be terrible."

Fargo decided that now was the time to be blunt. "How long have you been with the bank?"

"Six years. I was very good in arithmetic at the schoolhouse. Arithmetic and spelling and penmanship. So they hired me when I was sixteen. I'm the first person in my family to have a job in town. My folks are about twenty miles from here."

"They must be pretty proud of you."

"They are."

"And they'd sure hate to see you lose your job because you wouldn't go along with something that Mr. Ericson wanted you to say."

The cheeks flushed deep red once again. "I don't lie, Deputy Fargo."

"No?"

"No. And I resent what you're trying to say."

She started to walk away. To her back Fargo said, "There's a man's life at stake here, Amy. I just want to make sure you understand that."

She stopped, turned around. "I'm not a child. I understand what could happen to him. But I also understand that he's the killer. People saw him running away. Doesn't that tell you something? If he ran, then he had something to hide. Otherwise he would've gone and gotten the sheriff. I don't have anything personal against him. He made a terrible fool out of himself over Jane. I even felt a little sorry for him about that."

"Did you know Jane?"

"I knew her from church."

"Did you like her?"

"Everybody liked Jane."

"Does 'everybody' include you?"

A troubled smile. "If you're asking if I resented her because most of the available men spent half their time mooning over her—yes, I suppose I did. But it wasn't for anything she did. She wasn't flirtatious at all. She was a very serious young woman. And she had terrible luck with men."

Her remark startled Fargo. Jane the heartbreaker had bad luck with men? "I don't follow you."

"That's why she broke off her engagement to Ken, my boss. He cheated on her. She wanted to keep herself pure until their wedding night. He seemed to think this entitled him to stray a little bit. Only a man would be stupid enough to think that she'd put up with it. And no matter how careful they are, word always gets around."

"How about Frank Rhodes? How was their engagement going?"

"Fine," she said. "At least as far as I know."

Then she turned and walked away.

Rooney said, "The way you treated me today, Cawthorne, I should leave you right in this cell."

Of all the people to hear his call for help, Cawthorne thought as Rooney opened the cell door. Could have been damned near anybody. But no, it had to be Rooney. Who had to be enjoying the hell out of this. And who would be enjoying it doubly when he reported it to Standish. If they wanted even more proof that Cawthorne was now too old for the job, they certainly had it. A punk like Donlon taking away his gun and locking him in a cell. Cawthorne had been admired, hated and feared in this town. But for all the toes he'd stepped on he'd never been a laughingstock. Now he would be the town joke.

Rooney said, "I'll keep this between us. Shows you the kind of man I am."

"Sure you will, Rooney."

"That's what I get for trying to be decent?"

"Ten minutes from now, half the town'll know how stupid I was."

"Seems to me the thing we should be worryin' about is getting up a posse."

"Can't disagree with you there. You go round them up. Have them meet out front here as soon as possible."

"This time you won't have to worry about a lynchin', Sheriff. I promise you that."

"Open season on Donlon, huh?" Cawthorne said as the two men walked to the front of the building.

"Well, if this don't prove that he killed her, what does?"

"I have to say you're probably right about that. But shooting him down without a trial doesn't help matters."

Rooney grinned. "Saves time if nothing else." The smile grew mean. "Besides, I'd think you'd want to see the man who humiliated you lyin' on the ground with a flower in his hand."

"I can see you're gonna keep this just between us."

Rooney didn't even try to argue otherwise. He just walked to the rifle rack on the east wall, picked the proper key from the ring he carried and took down the rifle he wanted. "You sure you're up to goin' along on this? I can handle it the same way I did the other day. I brought him in, didn't I?"

"Fargo found him. You'd still be wandering around out there, probably out of water and lost except for Fargo."

Rooney frowned. "Oh, yes, your new deputy. A lot of folks don't like him much."

"'A lot of folks' meaning you and your cronies?"

"A lot of folks meaning the people who pay your salary."

"Uh-huh." He nodded to the door. "Thought you were in such a hurry to go round up a posse."

"Just wanted to let you know how people feel about Fargo. If I'm leading this posse, by the way, he ain't goin' along."

"You the new sheriff, are you?"

"I'm the one who hauled your ass out of that cell back there, ain't I?"

No way Cawthorne could argue with that. And no way he could argue with Rooney leading the posse. Cawthorne didn't have the energy. He couldn't even fake it.

"So when you see Fargo, you tell him he won't be ridin' with the posse, okay, Sheriff?"

Cawthorne was too worn out to argue. "I'll tell him, Rooney." Suddenly he felt bone fatigue. He lowered himself into a chair. "I'll tell him."

Rooney glanced at the weary, beaten old man in front of him and grinned. Sure was funny how fast things changed. Just a few hours ago he'd been damned near out of a job. Now he was more or less running the place.

Yeah, it sure was funny.

Skunk saw Fargo on the street and knew it was safe to go back to the barn again. He didn't like moving about in daylight. He didn't appreciate the things people said to him. Sometimes they were so mean he could barely move. He was frozen in place, stunned at how hateful they could be. So it was better just to stay away from human eyes.

The storage barn had different eyes watching him; some of them watched him fondly. The little black-and-white kitten he fed. The injured bird he was nursing back to health. The stray dog that came around once a day. Skunk always saved a few scraps from the food the café set out for him. The scraps he gave to the grateful mutt in exchange for a sloppy embrace. These were his friends and every once in a while they were all together in the hay in the back of the storage barn and those were the best times of all for Skunk.

But now his mind was on Frank Rhodes. Skunk knew that Rhodes was the killer. No doubt about it in his mind. No, he hadn't actually seen Rhodes kill her but when he woke up and saw Rhodes weaving drunkenly over the body, blood streaking his hands and arms in the golden moonlight—

Skunk knew it was time to leave this town. He had exhausted everybody's tolerance. That was the way he looked at it because that was the way it felt. The gibes had gotten increasingly hostile. The threats from the drunks at night had gotten increasingly violent. And the man who owned the barn, a Mr. Rutledge, had started warning him that Skunk couldn't sleep in the barn forever, that one of these days he would have to get out. . . . get out of town.

And that was where Frank Rhodes was going to help him. Rhodes had plenty of money. And easy access to greenbacks. He could get Skunk all the money he needed

tonight. And by dawn, Skunk would be gone. And in a little while, with the help of Rhodes's money, there would be a new Skunk, except he wouldn't be "Skunk" anymore; he'd use his real name and be his old respectable self, William Abner Cosgrove, Jr. And how he'd shine all cleaned up in new clothes and a gold-toothed smile. And there would be ladies and he didn't care if he had to pay for them, either. It had been so long, so damned long.

You could see that Skunk's daydreams had the effect of making him walk a little taller as he approached the barn. He was already a bit of William Abner Cosgrove, Jr., just thinking of what lay ahead for him.

He was hoping that the shadows inside the barn would cool him off some. But he was now several steps inside and the heat, if anything, seemed even more oppressive. Well, he hadn't given it enough time. He'd go back to the hay and lie down and probably by lying still he'd start the process of getting cooler—

The blow came from behind and without any warning at all. Skunk figured that nobody was more sensitive to the sights and sounds of the barn than he was because this had been his domain for some time.

But as his legs started to give way, as the blow to the back of his head started to send stunning pain across his skull, he realized that he hadn't heard a single sound. Whoever this was had managed to fool Skunk and Skunk didn't like that at all.

His last conscious thought was of how much more painful his ribs were than his head. He'd just been kicked in the ribs three, maybe four times.

And then came blessed darkness.

11

"One thing you better understand, Fargo," Rooney said, standing in front of the eight men who made up the posse. "I'm in charge. You take orders from me. I didn't really want to take you along, anyway."

Fargo could have made a pretty good argument for why this was a bad idea, namely that Rooney was a hotheaded show-off who was bound to make a big mistake sooner rather than later. The trouble was, these were special circumstances. Rooney, by freeing Cawthorne from his cell, had earned the right to lead the posse. At least that was how Rooney saw it, and since every man in the posse was a friend of Rooney's, they'd all back him up.

The riders were saddled up, eager to leave the front of the sheriff's office. A crowd had gathered. Another dramatic event for the gawkers. A woman, probably the wife of one of the posse members, was crying and dabbing her eyes while being comforted by another woman. They had reason to cry, Fargo thought cynically. They were all packing plenty of whiskey, he was sure of that, and they'd be drunk pretty quickly. They'd probably end up accidentally shooting each other.

"You hear what I'm tellin' you?" Rooney said, relishing his moment as boss.

"I hear you, Rooney. I just want to make sure Donlon doesn't get killed when he doesn't need to."

Rooney sneered. "Hear that, men? Fargo here is goin' along to protect Donlon." He turned back to Fargo. "How about us? You worried about us, Fargo? What if he opens fire on us?"

"Then you have a right to shoot him. I just don't want to see him shot in the back."

"We don't need him along, anyway," a man said. Fargo recognized him as one of the posse members he'd seen in the desert. He was the one who'd tried to cuff Fargo. The way Fargo had handled him, he probably hadn't made a friend. He was pretty sure he wouldn't be invited to the man's next birthday party.

"He shouldn't be wearin' no badge, anyway," snapped another man. "He ain't even from this town. This is something for us to settle, not no outsider."

All the men would have agreed but at the moment two of them were busy guzzling down whiskey from the pints they carried in their saddlebags. This was going to be one professional posse, no doubt about it, Fargo thought.

"Sounds like you got a lot of friends in this group, Fargo," Rooney said. "You ain't been here even a day yet and you got all sorts of people wantin' to push your face in for you."

"They're welcome to try, Rooney. And that includes you."

The posse members grinned. A fight. What could be a better way to launch a manhunt than have its leader involved in a fistfight? Or maybe even a gunfight. Yes, Fargo thought, a real crack professional posse, no doubt about it.

But the fight was forestalled when Cawthorne came out of the sheriff's office. "You men all got rifles?"

Most of the men held their rifles up for him to see.

"I've got an extra one in there if anybody needs it."

"We're all ready, Sheriff. I just want to make sure Fargo here understands that I'm in charge."

A helpless expression played on Cawthorne's face. "That's the way this has got to be, Fargo. You're still my deputy. But Rooney is taking the lead on this one."

"I understand, Sheriff."

As he spoke, Fargo saw past Rooney a familiar figure hurry toward the general store. He said to Rooney, "How long ago did you say Donlon escaped?"

"Who gives a damn how long ago he escaped? We're leavin' right now. And you can come along or stay. Don't

make no never mind to me." He walked over to his horse and climbed up into the saddle.

"I'd say about twenty, twenty-five minutes ago," Cawthorne said to Fargo.

Fargo suppressed a smile. Rounding up a posse in so little time meant one thing. Rather than pick the most qualified men, Rooney had raced over to one of the saloons nearby and filled his hand that way.

The twenty, twenty-five minutes also meant one other thing, something that Fargo didn't care to divulge right now. "You go on ahead. Probably a good idea if we aren't in the same posse, anyway."

Rooney laughed. "Now there's a wise man." He winked at the man nearest him. "Never know what can happen out there on that trail, do you? Fargo here could wind up getting shot himself."

His men made happy noises. A finer group of drunken bums Fargo had rarely seen.

As the posse left, a few of the women waved handkerchiefs at them. Little boys and little girls ran alongside the horses until they couldn't keep up. An old duffer said, "Donlon sure ain't comin' back alive." Everybody around him nodded in agreement.

But Fargo didn't pay much attention. He was still watching the familiar figure enter the general store. Now that was downright puzzling, Fargo thought. Though he had a pretty good idea what was going on in the general store right about now.

"Glad you didn't go with them," Cawthorne said. "Drunk as they'll be, they probably would've tried to kill you. Especially if they didn't have any luck with Donlon."

"Nice group of fellas Rooney hangs around with."

Cawthorne laughed. "Yeah, and Rooney himself bein' such a sterling character and all."

"Well, listen, Sheriff. Right now I'm going to do a little more investigating. I'll check in with you later."

"You're not goin' after Donlon?"

"In my way I'm going after him," Fargo said.

He didn't even wait around for the sheriff to say, "Huh?"

* * *

Somehow he had pissed his pants. It only added to the misery of his busted head and the chin damage he'd collected when he'd fallen facedown on the dirt floor of the barn. Skunk had yet to stand up. He didn't know if he had the strength. For now all he could do was stare at the fancy Wellington boot that was less than four inches from his nose.

"That's just a taste of what you'll be getting if you try playing any games with me," a male voice said. This would be Frank Rhodes, of course. The visit to his office and the snooty Miss Swinnerton had paid the wrong kind of dividends.

"I could kill you right here and right now. But I'm going to give you a chance to stay alive. Are you listening, Skunk?"

Skunk decided that now was probably a good time to get on his feet. But as soon as he started to sit up the pain in his ribs cut through him like a scimitar. He clutched his side. He was afraid he would pass out again. Tears came without warning and he fell again to the ground.

Then something dropped to the floor very near his face. When the pain had faded somewhat, he opened one eye and gaped at the thick white business envelope Rhodes had let fall.

"Get up and open it."

"I—can't, Mr. Rhodes. My ribs hurt too much."

"I'll kick them again if you don't get up."

"Oh please, Mr. Rhodes—"

"You shouldn't have been so stupid, Skunk. You don't have the intelligence to do something like this and now you're paying the price. Now sit up before I start kicking you again."

Skunk knew there was no way he could comply without inflicting massive pain on himself. Was there anything more painful than bruised or broken ribs? He didn't know which he suffered from at the moment but it didn't matter. Both were the kind of pain nobody should have to endure.

He cried; he cursed; his left fist pounded the ground; he came to his feet inch by groaning inch. But somehow he

stood up, though he knew he was near to just falling down unconscious again.

"You forgot to pick up the envelope."

"Oh, no, Mr. Rhodes. Don't make me—"

"I should make you do it, Skunk. That way you'd realize that you can't handle this sort of thing at all. There's four hundred dollars in that envelope but you're so stupid you just let it lay there on the floor."

"No, please, Mr. Rhodes—"

"But being the good fellow I am—" He bent down and picked up the envelope. When he stood straight again, he stared at Skunk, a very sleek man he was, and said, "There are two tickets in here. One for the stage. It leaves in two hours. It'll take you to the capital. That's where you can use the second ticket. That'll get you on a train for St. Louis. And you'll have four hundred dollars to spend. You can change your whole life with four hundred dollars. You'll have new clothes and you can get a sleeping room and start looking around for a job. I don't know what turned you into the kind of man you are now but I'm giving you an opportunity nobody else would. You understand me?"

Skunk could see that Rhodes thought he was really doing him a substantial favor. And he seemed genuine about Skunk starting a new life. Of course, Mr. Rhodes was doing all this for his own sake. He didn't want Skunk around to identify him to anybody. The problem was Skunk's dream had been much bigger than a four-hundred-dollar dream. His had been at least a two- or three-thousand-dollar dream. Now *there* was a dream. Four hundred just didn't seem like much—

"You'd be a fool not to take this, Skunk."

A four-hundred-dollar dream? No. That wasn't good enough for Skunk, that was for sure. But if he balked, he had no doubt what Mr. Rhodes would do to him. Maybe his ribs weren't broken—maybe they were only bruised—but if he balked, Mr. Rhodes was sure to start kicking them again until they were broken for sure.

"So what about it, Skunk? Is your answer yes or no?"

"Well, I really appreciate this, Mr. Rhodes. I really do." He winced as he spoke. "I'll take the envelope for sure."

Rhodes, standing there sleek and nervously handsome, beamed like a boy who'd just received a wonderful gift. "That's very sensible of you, Skunk," he said, handing over the envelope. "Remember now, the stage leaves in two hours."

12

Three elderly men stood on the sidewalk in front of the general store. They watched the last of the posse members ride away. They wished they were young enough to be in a posse. They remembered their own youth, tracking down killers in the earliest of frontier times. It was probably an unholy thing to admit but stalking a human was a lot more interesting than stalking an animal, even a bear. Because the human could shoot back. Funny how some humans took to danger just the way others took to complete safety.

Their attention left the posse and focused on the man approaching them. Why wasn't *he* with the posse? Sheriff Cawthorne had given him a badge; why wasn't he using it? What the hell was he doing heading for the general store when the real men were out hunting down a killer?

Two of the men were about to say something sly to him—something that would indicate they didn't think he was much of a man—but as he drew closer and they got a better look at his face they decided that they'd better keep quiet. There was a stony resolve in the eyes that looked to be right on the edge of anger. He carried himself easy enough but you sensed that he could turn into a fighting animal in seconds. Maybe he was even the kind to strike an old duffer if that old duffer said something he didn't like.

So they let him pass. He walked up onto the sidewalk, nodded hello to them and proceeded on into the store.

"I figured you'd say something to him," said one of the old men.

"Hell, I thought *you* were gonna say something. That's why *I* didn't say nothing."

It was an argument that would go on the rest of the day, one man blaming the other for not speaking up to Fargo and telling the new deputy exactly what they thought of a man who wouldn't join a posse.

Inside, Fargo pretended to be interested in a stack of work shirts. Yes, indeed, had there ever been a human being more interested in work shirts than Skye Fargo? Unlikely, considering the spellbound way he picked one up and thoroughly assessed it. He probably *dreamed* of work shirts, he was so fanatically fascinated by them.

What he was really doing, of course, was watching the elegant redhead Grace Donlon stuff items into her wicker shopping basket. She worked quickly. Right now she was putting three cans of beans in the basket. She'd just finished dropping a hefty supply of jerky in there. Basics, that was what she was stocking up on.

She was so intent on what she was doing that she hadn't noticed Fargo come in. Which was fine with Fargo, now that he knew what she was doing. What he'd suspected she was up to as soon as he'd seen her entering this store.

When he got back outside, the old men were gone. He'd seen the contempt in their eyes. It had been obvious that at least one of them had wanted to say something to him but had decided that that was risky. Fargo smiled about that. *Yep, there's nothing I enjoy more than beating the hell out of people over eighty. Not much more satisfaction in life than that.*

The wicker basket was so full of groceries the lid wouldn't close. Grace came out of the store and stood for a moment on the landing, looking left, looking right. And looking very guilty about it all. Then she set off in the direction of the Donlon family home on the edge of town. The sun was still flexing its muscles, pounding everything below it into complete submission, making everybody wish they had a root cellar where they could hide all day. Even if it did smell of the grave, a root cellar would be a whole lot better than this.

Fargo gave Grace Donlon a few minutes' head start and then began following her. He stopped when he came within sight of the one-story adobe house that was set off by itself.

The grounds were tidy, indicating pride and care. Grace went inside quickly.

He had to give Bryce Donlon credit. Here a posse of eight overeager men was racing across the countryside in search of him and he was sitting right at home.

His time had come.

Don Jackson had been out working on his farm when a neighbor stopped by and told him about the posse Clyde Rooney was getting up. Jackson had missed the last couple of posses because he'd been working so hard.

As his neighbor was telling him about the posse, Jackson's gaze strayed to his son, Mark. The boy, smart as he was, was also good at physical labor and he liked helping his father work on the farm.

As usual when his eyes touched on the boy, he felt the torment of the lie he'd been living with since Mark's birth. He'd been gone for a few months to St. Louis back then and when he returned Sarah was radiant—but strangely anxious—about her pregnancy. The first he'd heard about it, of course. There was no question that it was his child. At least that was the way she treated it. And he wasn't about to disappoint her with certain questions. She'd lost two other babies in miscarriages. This was a time for happiness. He forced himself to believe that the questions he had were only the doubts of a jealous and mistrustful man for a woman everybody said was a model of faithfulness and honor.

But in Mark's second year certain facial characteristics became painfully apparent. When he looked at the boy, he saw, unmistakably, the face of Clyde Rooney.

Rooney had been a family friend until he'd started showing up at the house when Jackson wasn't home. Sarah assured Jackson that the calls had simply been friendly ones and that Rooney, who hadn't been married at the time, had been asking advice about a woman at church he said he was interested in romantically.

Jackson found a way to pick a fight with Rooney shortly after a visit. They'd been drinking an evening away and Jackson suddenly accused him of stealing a saddle that

Jackson kept in a shed back of the house. Rooney said he was crazy. Jackson then proceeded to remind Rooney with his fists that not only did Jackson possess Sarah, he also possessed far superior fighting skills.

The problem wasn't only that Mark wasn't his blood son; Don Jackson had come to love the boy despite himself. He was a good boy and a boon companion for fishing, hunting and working around the farm.

But Jackson knew that he wouldn't be able to feel at peace with himself as long as Rooney was alive. He couldn't stand it when they went to town and he saw Rooney and Sarah exchange glances. He couldn't stand it at church when Rooney helped take up the collection and always had a smile for Sarah. He did these things to spite Jackson and Jackson knew it.

He'd never confronted Sarah about any of this, not even the fact that he knew that Mark wasn't his own. He didn't want Sarah to leave him. He hated himself for his weakness but there it was. He had seen men who couldn't survive the loss of a wife leaving and he was secretly afraid that that would be his fate, too.

So he settled for ridding himself of demons by ridding himself—and the world—of Clyde Rooney.

And not until today and this posse had Don Jackson seen such an opportunity to bid a final good-bye to the man who was the real father of Jackson's son.

13

Fargo walked a half block down from the Donlon house, then worked his way back so he could get a good look at the yard where startlingly white wash hung on the clotheslines. An unsaddled horse stood there. Grace wouldn't have been foolish enough to saddle it. Too easy to figure out what was going on.

Fargo figured the easiest way in was the back door. Probably wasn't locked. And it was a small enough house that wherever Bryce was hiding, he wouldn't be hard to find.

Fargo went up to the back door. From then on he walked on tiptoe. He eased open the door, unlocked as he'd suspected, and went inside. Smells of beef stew and fresh bread made him hungry. But the undertone of conversation made him alert. They were in the next room.

Fargo drew his Colt and proceeded inward.

When Bryce saw him, he leapt from his chair as if he were spring-loaded. In any other circumstances, it would have been funny. A rifle leaned against the wall nearby and that was what Bryce was reaching for.

"No, Bryce!" Grace said.

"Your sister's right, Bryce. Don't make me shoot you."

But if Fargo thought he had an ally in Grace, he was wrong. Even though Bryce fell back in his chair, Grace snapped at Fargo, "I thought you were a better man than that, Fargo. I thought you were interested in who really killed poor Jane. But you're throwing in with the rest of them and blaming Bryce. I'd rather have you kill me than turn him over to Rooney and his cronies."

"I didn't kill her, Fargo," Bryce said. "I really didn't."

Fargo smiled. "You were smart. What'd you do, let the horse you stole from the jail just go on ahead of you so they'd follow it?"

But Bryce was in no smiling mood. He just nodded.

"But they're going to be back in town pretty soon and they're going to head right for here."

"That's why I'm stuffing everything I can into saddlebags," Grace said. "So he can get a head start on them and have plenty of food and water to escape."

"There's more of them and they're pretty hard-nosed. He might escape but if I had to bet I'd bet against it. Those boys want him pretty bad."

"But he didn't do it."

Fargo said, "I'm going to surprise you and tell you that I at least think that's a possibility."

Sister and brother looked at each other in disbelief.

"Do you really mean that?" she said.

"Yeah, and I'll tell you why."

He then reported the conversations he'd had in the last few hours. "That doesn't mean that Bryce isn't guilty. But it raises some interesting questions. Ericson had a reason to kill her—anger that she'd pushed him over for Rhodes. And Rhodes—for all we know something had gone wrong with their relationship. I want to ask a few of her friends about that. But right now the thing is to get Bryce back in jail."

"No!" Donlon cried. "Don't let him take me, Sis! Please! They'll lynch me tonight for sure."

She touched Fargo's arm. "You can't do this, Skye. He's right. They'll come after him for sure. Standish will pay them if he has to. Everybody in the mob will be trying to please Standish. That's how things work around here."

Fargo understood their fear. There probably would be an attempt to lynch him. But by breaking out of jail Bryce had only convinced people with open minds that he was guilty. Now he had to show them that he was innocent by going back to jail. He had to stand up to the legal system and submit himself to it.

"Don't let him, Sis. Don't let him," Bryce said from his chair. He was almost whimpering, childlike.

Fargo faced Grace. He was within inches of her. In most circumstances he would take her in his arms right here and right now. But obviously this wasn't the time. "We have to trust the law. It's the only hope he's got. Say he does escape. Standish will hunt him down till he finds him. It might take years but Standish has the money and the anger. He'll keep paying Pinkertons till they find him. And he'll pay the Pinkertons to shoot to kill. He won't be satisfied with bringing Bryce back. He'll want an assassination on the spot. Is that how you want to live, Bryce?"

"Right now that sounds a hell of a lot better than being lynched."

"You could let him go, Skye. You don't have to tell anybody you found him here."

For a moment Fargo wavered. Maybe she was right. Maybe that was the best thing to do. Maybe he and Cawthorne wouldn't be able to hold off the mob. Maybe they'd get to Bryce. Maybe they'd lynch Bryce. And maybe because of all those points . . . just maybe he should do what Grace said and let Bryce go.

But, no. He wore a badge, for one thing. He owed Cawthorne loyalty to his office. And for another, Bryce might be a troublemaker but that didn't make him a skilled outlaw. Fargo had no doubt that the posse would find Bryce and kill him on the spot.

"You're coming back with me," Fargo said. "And I'd advise you to make it easy for both of us. No sense in you getting hurt."

Fargo could see the resignation on Grace's face. "He's right, Bryce. We have to do what he says. He's the law now."

"But they'll—" Bryce didn't bother to finish his sentence. He'd said everything so many times it was useless at this point to repeat it all again. He did believe he'd be lynched. But in truth he didn't have the energy needed to flee. Maybe if he'd had eight hours of good sleep and some healthy food—maybe then he would feel up to trying to elude the posse. But right now—No, even though he was terrified of going back to jail, there was no point in arguing with Fargo anymore.

Bryce stood up. His entire body trembled. He thought his legs would give out. He was aware of his sister's look of concern and fear. If only the rest of this town was so understanding . . .

"I think we should be leaving now," Fargo said gently to Grace. "I want to get him in his cell as quick as I can. There won't be a lot of people in the street right now and that'll help us."

Grace went to her brother, embraced him. For a long time she just held him the way she would a child. Fargo was both embarrassed and moved by what he saw.

When she let him go, she turned to Fargo. "I'm counting on you to protect him."

"You don't have to worry about that. Anybody tries anything, they'll have to kill me first. And Cawthorne'll be the same way."

She nodded.

Outside, the sun still poured pain on the town. Some wag had once noted that heat wore you out faster than making love. Yes, Fargo thought, and it wasn't half as much fun.

The two men were connected by the handcuff on Fargo's left wrist and Donlon's right. Donlon still complained about the handcuff. Said he didn't need it. Said he could be trusted. Fargo smiled. Donlon was naive about this whole thing. Somehow he expected people just to take his word for it that he was innocent. And that bolting jail was just what anybody would do. And so he balked at being handcuffed, as if this was a major offense to his good nature and reputation.

"You're a wanted man, Donlon. You better keep that in mind."

"I'm an innocent man. You said so yourself."

"That's not what I said and you know it. I said that there are a couple of other men I think should be questioned before any decision is made about who killed Jane Standish. That's a lot different from saying you're innocent."

Obviously, Donlon had created this fantasy in which Fargo had declared him innocent. And now that Fargo was setting him straight, he started sulking.

When they reached the business district, a few dozen

eyes took note of their progress toward the sheriff's office. Even elderly ladies stopped to watch them. Men nudged each other, nodded in the direction of the new deputy and the Donlon boy. They were trying to figure out how the new deputy had managed to capture Donlon already. And when they realized what had happened . . . their faces broke into slow, ironic smiles. And somewhere out in the distance you had Rooney and all his blustery, boisterous posse looking for Bryce Donlon . . . and Bryce Donlon was right here.

If everything was settled and done—if Skunk had surely been sensible and used the money to get out of town— then why was Frank Rhodes so damnably nervous?

He sat in his office in an agony of grief and misery. He had always been a believer in the luck of his family. Just about everything they attempted turned out well. But luck ran out somewhere along the line, didn't it? Wasn't there someone in the family line who was notably *un*lucky? And wasn't *he* the one who always got talked about—the unlucky one?

Tried for murder. Now there would be something for future generations to talk about. Yessir, the luck of the Rhodes family held tight right up until—

Miss Swinnerton knocked. "I bought some scented candles. Bayberry. They smell very sweet. The outer office is livable again."

"Thank you, Miss Swinnerton."

She studied him with one of her most severe gazes. "Did he upset you, sir? If some of his odor stuck to your clothes, I'll be happy to give you the cleanser I use and—"

"No, no, he didn't upset me."

"I'm just surprised he had the gall to come here."

Miss Swinnerton wanted to know what had brought Skunk here. This was her way of trying to get him to at least hint at the reason.

"He was mistaken, was all. Fool's errand."

"Coming from a fool, I'm not surprised."

"Just so, Miss Swinnerton."

"I can bring one of the candles in here if you'd like."

"No, that won't be necessary, Miss Swinnerton."

"Very well, Mr. Rhodes. I'll leave you alone then."

But he could tell she was curious about why he was so disturbed, why he was so seemingly paralyzed. He hadn't gotten much work done since Skunk's odd appearance. Then he'd suddenly fled from the office for a time, returning not long ago to sit in his office chair and stare. And to wring his hands. And sigh deeply. And to make little distressed sounds that were trapped in his throat. What could that terrible Skunk have said that could have devastated Mr. Rhodes this way?

She decided that she never should have announced Skunk. She should have turned him right back out on the street. And if he'd offered any trouble, she should have looked for that new deputy that Henry Cawthorne had sworn in this morning. He certainly wouldn't have had any trouble tossing Skunk out. Might even have tossed him right into a jail cell where he belonged.

It was rare for Miss Swinnerton to admit to a failure but now that she thought about it, yes, she had indeed failed her employer. She should never have let Skunk see him.

After Miss Swinnerton exited, Rhodes went back to considering the ultimate problem—that being, what if Skunk didn't leave town? What if he didn't think the money was enough? What if he stayed on to continue demanding more and more money?

After the first kill . . . the others come easy.

Rhodes had once represented a man who'd told him that. The first kill . . . you weren't sure you could do it. You know, actually take the life of another human being. But after you got done with that first one . . . each successive one came easier. So that if you did enough of them . . . He'd smiled at Rhodes and said: "Well, you reach a certain number and it's no problem at all. You barely even think about it."

Rhodes had been happy to lose the case. The man was put to death, as he so richly deserved. That had been the only execution Rhodes had ever attended. He wanted to make sure that the man was in fact dead. That the man would never tread the earth again.

But now Rhodes was thinking thoughts very much like those of that killer—

Could Skunk be the first-time kill for Rhodes?

And then he thought bitterly: *But he'll be number two, won't he?*

Poor Jane had been number one.

14

"Never hurts a man to be humbled." Sheriff Cawthorne smiled after he'd safely locked Bryce Donlon in his cell. "And if this doesn't humble Rooney, I don't know what will." He enjoyed the thought of Rooney, all bluster and bravado, leading a posse for a man who sat in a jail cell. Rooney wasn't likely to see the humor in it, but then Rooney didn't see the humor in much.

"I'm glad you sent the rider, though," Fargo said. "Maybe he can catch the posse before they get too far."

"Rooney's probably gonna take it out on you."

Fargo shrugged. "I guess that's one run-in that's kind of inevitable, Sheriff. We took a big dislike to each other out there in the desert. I guess we're both kind've sorry that we haven't been able to do anything about it yet."

They were in the front office now. Cawthorne was in his chair, boots up on the desk. Fargo was perched on the edge of the other desk. "So you think there's a chance that Bryce didn't kill her?"

"A chance. And that's all there is. There're still witnesses who saw him running away from there. That makes him a pretty good suspect, but it doesn't mean he actually killed her. Maybe what he said is true. He found her, got scared and ran. That's logical enough."

"We never found out who she was meeting in the head of that alley."

"Not yet. She came into town to see somebody at nine o'clock. All she told her folks was that she would be back soon. That's what Mr. Standish told you, correct?"

Cawthorne nodded. "What about Ken Ericson and Rhodes? They claimed they had alibis."

"Neither one of their alibis will hold up. Ericson's secretary knows something she hasn't told me yet but I have a feeling it's about his alibi. And Rhodes said he didn't see her at all that night. That he was working in his office."

"And nobody saw him?"

"That's what he says. I think he thinks that the Rhodes name will get him through. Nobody will challenge him because of his old man."

"Well, Fargo, then he isn't counting on how crazy Standish is right now. He doesn't give a damn who he hurts. He just wants revenge. And right now he thinks that means Bryce Donlon. If you think you can turn up anything on these other two, you better do it damned quick while we still got time." He sat up now. "This day isn't over yet."

"I know."

"Most likely the posse'll be back in a few hours and they'll be wanting something in return for going off half-cocked the way they did. The first place Rooney should have looked was Grace Donlon's home. But that wouldn't have involved any gunplay so it didn't interest him. But now Rooney and the others'll be ready to save face. They'll want to prove what big, bad men they are. And there's only one good way to do that now."

"Lynch Donlon."

"That's right."

"I don't suppose you've had any luck recruiting any more deputies."

Cawthorne snorted. "And go up against Standish? Everybody's afraid of him. If he can't fire them he can get somebody to foreclose on them. Whatever it takes, he can run them out of this town damned fast. And there won't be anything anybody can do about it, either."

"Be nice to have that much power—or maybe not. Maybe I'd just misuse it the same way most men do."

Cawthorne said, "That sure seems to be how it goes, don't it?"

They were silent for a time. Fargo couldn't help but

laugh. "I just keep picturing Rooney's face when that rider tells him that Donlon is already in jail."

"I got to admit, I'd pay to see his face, too. He is gonna be one mad mustang, I'll tell you that."

"Yeah," Fargo said, "I can picture him right now."

Every time Rooney glanced over his shoulder, he noticed that Don Jackson was staring right at him. Gave Rooney the shivers, actually. Had good, old, stupid Don figured out that the boy Mark wasn't his?

That question was particularly pressing now because Rooney, Jackson and a man named Paul Givens had separated from the others and were now facing pinyon and juniper trees on a north-facing slope. A man could hide out in an area like this for a long time. And a man could find himself in possession of a hell of a good site for opening fire on three men stupid enough to stand around in the open.

Rooney said, "I think we should split up and head into those trees. He could be watching us right now."

"Where's his horse?" Givens said. He was a tough former miner who'd lost three fingers on his left hand. You could tell by the way he assessed both Rooney and Jackson that they didn't measure up to his standards of manhood. Not even close.

"He probably hid it."

Givens scowled. "Horses make noise, Rooney. Unless he's way the hell up there, we'd have heard something in this heat. You know how horses are."

Jackson couldn't see much sense in Givens's argument but he enjoyed seeing Rooney goaded this way.

"You don't worry about no horse, Givens. I'm in charge here."

For the first time Jackson realized how drunk Givens was. He'd been gunning from a couple of pint bottles since they'd left town. "Oh, sure. Big, tough lawman. Big, tough punk, if you ask me. You want to throw down, do it right now, Rooney. You're taller'n me and fifteen years younger but I'd still pound you into the ground."

Givens had been insulting Rooney since they'd left town. Seemed that Rooney had once run Givens in for being

drunk and argumentative on a public street. Rooney had seemed to have forgotten the incident. Givens, however, couldn't seem to let go of it.

"I can't afford to pick a fight with you, Rooney. You might run me in the way you did that night last year when I was just havin' me a little fun with some friends. And you said I was this threat to the public well-being or some marble-mouthed piece of crap like that."

"I sure wish you'd forget that, Givens. I was just doin' my duty. It wasn't anything personal."

"Maybe not to you it wasn't. But to me—"

Jackson was almost shocked at the hatred he saw in Givens's eyes. This was a man who nursed his grudges to the point of insanity. But that was going to come in damned handy. Jackson could "accidentally" kill Rooney and he wouldn't have any trouble getting Givens to stand up for him. He wouldn't have any trouble at all.

"All right, Givens, you work that slope over there. I'll go right straight up this rise and Jackson, you move over to the east there. You understand?"

Givens snorted. "No. We don't understand, Rooney. We're too dumb to understand, ain't we, Jackson?"

Jackson had to smile. He enjoyed seeing Rooney being ragged on this way. For a drunk, Givens sure had a sharp, quick tongue.

But Rooney was sick of it and walked away, setting about the job he'd designated for himself.

Jackson stood there and watched him start working his way upslope between the trees and the heavy underbrush. A man could be hiding just about anywhere in those trees, especially with the sun starting its downward course.

This was going to be a lot easier than Jackson had thought. He knew his time was at hand. The time he'd waited all these years for.

Very soon now Clyde Rooney was going to pay for his sins. Very soon now Clyde Rooney was going to be dead.

15

Tyler Rhodes put down his pen and leaned back in his office chair and felt the sting of tears in his fifty-three-year-old eyes. He had never been as rich or powerful as Theodore Standish. But he had been rich and powerful enough to have his way just about every time he wanted it. And there had been only occasional rivalries between the two men. Most of the time they got on fine and worked well together on projects that benefited the town.

But now—

But now he was neither rich nor powerful enough to save his son from the reality of what he'd done to Jane Standish in that alley the other night.

And the next day he hadn't even remembered staggering into his parents' house, blood all over his arms and face and shirt. They'd cleaned him up, taken him home so he could get up and go to work in the morning as if nothing was wrong at all.

But now—

If Bryce Donlon wasn't lynched tonight there just might be time enough for Henry Cawthorne and his new deputy, Fargo, to start asking more questions—and coming up with some very uncomfortable answers.

He wiped his eyes as he heard somebody coming down the corridor that led to his office on the first floor of his mansion. The steps were too young and crisp to be his wife's. He decided they had to belong to Robert, that inscrutable Norwegian butler his wife had imported from St. Louis.

The one-knuckle knock. Sharp as a bullet. And the word: "Sir?"

"Yes, Robert."

"I'm sorry to trouble you, sir, but there's this—man— who insists on seeing you. I wouldn't advise letting him in the house, sir. I tried to shoo him away but he just keeps coming back and saying that you'll be 'very, very sorry' if you don't talk to him."

Rhodes was grateful. He was beginning to feel imprisoned by himself, by his own fears and dreads. A visitor would distract him, at least temporarily. The day was beginning to cool. It would be good to be outside.

When he reached the wide porch, he hesitated, staring down the steps at the least expected person who'd ever come calling on him. The man's name was Skunk, and a more addled and disreputable figure the town had never known. Rhodes, a cleanly man, winced even at this distance from seeing the encrusted filth on Skunk's clothes.

Rhodes's eyes lifted momentarily, taking in the sweep of lawn, the statuary his wife had brought back from her last trip to Europe. His life had been so pleasant, so serene until a few days ago. And somehow having Skunk standing at the bottom of the steps symbolized how severely things had changed. Rhodes sensed that he had lost control of his life suddenly.

"How can I help you?" Rhodes said, not moving from his place on the porch.

"I hate to bother you but I want to talk to you."

"Then talk, sir. Nobody's stopping you."

"I'm not sure we should talk in the open like this."

"We're alone here."

Skunk looked craftily about. "But you never know who might be listening."

What kind of foolish business had he gotten himself into? Rhodes wondered. He should have let Robert toss this man off the property. Robert was surprisingly physical for a seemingly reserved butler. He seemed to enjoy physical battle. He'd once tossed a rowdy, drunken cowhand off the premises.

"So what are you suggesting?"

"There's a nice gazebo over there."

"Yes, there is."

"Maybe we could sit in there."

Rhodes sighed. Crazier and crazier. Sit in the gazebo. The more he gave in to this man, the worse things would get. "I'm very busy, Mr.—" He realized he didn't know the man's real name. He couldn't call him Mr. Skunk, could he? "I need to get back to my work."

"This is about your son. I saw something the other night."

A long time ago, on a beery night in a border town, when Rhodes had been a young and reckless man, he'd been shot in the arm in a gunfight. He still remembered the shock of the bullet ripping into his flesh and bone. It was a sensation he would never forget. Skunk's mention of his son—and the ominous words "I saw something the other night"—had the same effect on him as the bullet wound. He felt weak, old, helpless.

"The gazebo," Rhodes managed to say. "Don't say another word till we get there."

Rhodes walked alone. When Skunk tried to draw near, Rhodes shook him off the way he would a vagrant dog. He could never remember loathing a man as much as he did this one at this moment. His son's future in the hands of a repellent misfit like this one?

The gazebo was octagonal shaped. Rhodes went in first, sat in his rocking chair. Skunk followed, sensing that the farther he sat from Rhodes, the happier Rhodes would be. He sat on a bench long enough for three people. He said, "Your son hurt me pretty bad."

Rhodes saw now that Skunk favored his right side and did a lot of wincing and eye blinking. Pain.

"I'm sure he had good reason."

"He thought he did. He thought he could get rid of me easy." From inside his filthy suit coat he pulled a long envelope and threw it on the slatted floor. "Train ticket and some money."

Rhodes didn't need the rest of the situation explained to him. "And you of course want more money."

"You would, too, Mr. Rhodes. In my situation, I mean."

Rhodes was Rhodes once again. His self-pity, even his fear, were gone now. He assessed this shambling man in front of him and decided that he had to be dealt with like the most threatening of business competitors.

"Exactly what did you see?"

"You know what I saw."

"No, I don't."

"I saw him kill her."

"Describe it to me."

"What?"

"Describe the killing to me. You said you saw him kill her. Exactly what happened?"

"Well—"

"You didn't see him kill her, did you?"

Skunk fell silent. Then, "He killed her."

"Where were you?"

"It was hot in the barn. I was sleepin' in the alley, the way I do sometimes."

"But you didn't actually see him kill her."

"When I woke up I seen him kneelin' over her and he had this bloody knife in his hands. He was bloody all over his hands and his shirt."

Rhodes once again fell into despair. Maybe Skunk hadn't witnessed the murder—not exactly—but kneeling over her with a bloody knife? Try that on for size in a court of law. A rich young man a jury wouldn't like on general principle—a town creature like Skunk saying what he'd just said to Rhodes—and no matter how much Skunk might be discredited by the defense attorney, you would probably get a conviction.

"You said Frank offered you money."

"And a train ticket."

"You were a fool not to take it."

"Chances like this don't come around very often for people like me."

"You were also a fool to come here."

Skunk smiled coyly. "You got more money than he does. Least that's what I figure."

Tyler Rhodes didn't carry a regulation pistol. Businessmen in the East rarely did and those were the men he

99

admired most, the Eastern ones with their good manners and sleek style. But that didn't stop him from carrying the derringer that he now took from inside his coat.

"Very foolish," was all he said before he stood up and walked over to Skunk and shot him dead.

16

Too bad the weather wasn't as chilly as Amy Tolliver's greeting, Fargo thought when she opened the door and said, "You have no right to be here."

"I want to find out where your boss was the night of the murder."

"You heard what he said. That's good enough for me."

She'd had time to think it over, Fargo knew. Between the time he'd seen her in the street, when she'd seemed more cooperative—between then and now she'd realized that disagreeing with her boss would, at the least, cost her job. And given his influence, he might be able to make her leave town.

"We need to talk," he said and pushed past her.

Her apartment was comprised of two large rooms heavily decorated with rugs and full drapes and the massive furniture, including the horsehair couch, that was currently fashionable. But for all its currency, the place still had the feel of what it was—a furnished apartment rented by the month.

The blond hair, the slender body, the anxiety still somehow managed to create an odd kind of erotic quality. Maybe it was the slight overbite. Or the small but full mouth. Or the gray eyes that hinted at the kind of loneliness that could be alleviated by sex.

Whatever it was, Fargo felt the tension that comes with the first inkling of conscious desire. He noticed the way her thin, white cotton blouse draped just so over her small but pleasing breasts, the way her hips swayed as she now walked ahead of him. And the perfume she wore was only more of an enhancement of what he read in her eyes.

She sat primly on a loveseat. He took a chair across from her. "You don't seem the kind who'd lie for a murderer."

"If you're trying to shock me, you're not succeeding. Mr. Ericson isn't a murderer."

"You know that for sure?"

"Yes, I do."

"You seem pretty sure of yourself."

"I read books, Mr. Fargo. Something you probably *don't* do. I read books and I learn about human nature."

Another sure sign of her loneliness. He pictured her sitting by her fancy lamp at night reading through the current fashionable novel. He also pictured her as the girl in school who was so studious that the boys, despite her quiet good looks, shunned her.

He said, "I read a book once." He smiled. "I sort of liked it."

She watched him as he spoke. Responding to his sarcasm, she smiled too. "I suppose I did sound a little grand here."

"I probably don't look like much of a reader. That's understandable."

She sighed. "Lord, I don't want to get involved in this. I don't want to lie but I do want to keep my job."

"That's understandable, too. But there's a man sitting in jail—"

"He killed her."

"How do you know that?"

"Well, everybody says so."

"The sheriff doesn't say so."

"Well, he's—old." Then she made a face. "I'm sorry. You see what I'm doing? I'm trying to protect myself. If Bryce Donlon's guilty, then what I say or don't say doesn't matter."

"So your boss was lying."

She leaned back in the loveseat. Closed her eyes momentarily. "I didn't walk him to Beth's house if that's what you mean. But that doesn't make him a killer."

"No, but it does make him a liar."

"Everybody tells little lies."

"This isn't 'little.' "

She put her small face in her small hands and began

crying. Fargo froze. He was never sure what to do with women who cried in front of him. Sometimes they were just trying to manipulate him. But most of the time they were caught up in whatever problem they had and the grief was genuine.

"I don't want to lose my job," she said between sobs.

Without realizing what he was doing, Fargo stood up and walked over to the loveseat, sitting himself down next to her. He could smell her perfume mixed with the scent of her warm tears. She allowed herself to lean against him, her face nuzzled into the side of his neck.

They both felt the same helpless charge of passion that made what happened next inevitable. Her tears drying on his neck, she raised her small face up to Fargo and kissed him tenderly on the lips. All her anger, all her misgivings had left her and she was now offering herself to Fargo as a simple, trusting woman who wanted the respite from the world that only sex could offer.

Fargo swept her up in his arms and carried her to her bed. Her golden hair spread out behind her as he slowly began undoing the buttons on the front of her blouse. As she helped him relieve her of her clothes, he began kissing her small but perfectly formed breasts and taking in the sweet muskiness of her womanliness. She writhed against him as the last of the buttons were worked free. His fingers found her and she began to moan and work against his hand. Now she helped him rid himself of his trousers so that she could take in his manly size and hold it against her breasts. She held his staff reverently, as if it were a religious icon of some kind, and then she began flicking at it with her tongue.

Fargo slowly slid down her stomach, every inch of him seeming to excite her more and more until he too was in a frenzy of need that only entering her seemed to quell. She accepted him with a passion that was almost alarming. It was a kind of madness that he soon fell into himself as she reared and bucked and twisted to take him ever deeper into her.

In the middle of it all, she eased him out so she could roll over and he could enter her from the back of her wom-

anliness. Fargo grabbed her slender hips and began to pound home the power she so obviously wanted to feel from him.

By the end of it, when they fell facedown next to each other on her bed, they were spent following the brief and almost violent exchange of juices and passions they had just enjoyed.

Fargo sighed secretly to himself. Playing detective wasn't a bad job at all. You met some very interesting ladies in the course of your investigation.

As the purple shadows began to lengthen across the desert, as the night creatures began to survey the battleground they would face tonight, Don Jackson saw the first opportunity he'd had to shoot and kill Clyde Rooney.

But he pushed his demons away momentarily so he could enjoy the lingering death of daylight. Nothing was more beautiful than the desert at dawn and dusk. An otherworldly feeling always came over him, as if he had been transported to one of the planets he saw at night when he stood in his backyard on the farm. There was a hush now, a sense of peace that only the desert could give him. Even the bighorn sheep down on the plateau were affected by the melancholy of it all, lying down tranquilly as the sky faded from blue to the streaked colors of gold and rust and purple before becoming a rich dark blue.

But he could never keep his demons away long. Especially not the demon named Rooney.

From where he stood on the rise, he could see Rooney searching the trees down below. He had slowly been moving across the rise so that he would be in position when the time was right. His story would be simple enough. He spotted somebody he took to be Bryce Donlon. He shouted twice to the man to give himself up. But the man wouldn't respond. He just kept moving through the trees. After a third such warning, Jackson felt justified in starting to fire. Not until he was able to see the man—now dead—close up did he realize what a terrible mistake he'd made. He'd killed Clyde Rooney.

He didn't have to worry about a groundswell of support for Rooney in town. Rooney was a bully and a braggart

and had managed to offend a large number of citizens. Few would say it but the common sentiment would be "Good riddance."

Jackson had never killed a man before. Anticipating it, he felt a strange combination of desire and fear. Could he actually do it? As much as he despised Rooney, he still had to wonder when the time actually came—

Rooney had found a narrow path leading to the top of the rise. Making things easier for Jackson. All he had to do was take his rifle and pump a couple of bullets into the man. And that would be that.

Jackson leaned against a pinyon tree, drawing a careful bead on his target. A very easy shot, really. He fought down panic. He wished his rage would take over. But he couldn't get to his rage for some reason. All he could find within himself now was anxiety about taking another man's life.

But he was going to do it. He was sure he was. He was just going to give Rooney a little more time to work his way up the path and then—

At first, Jackson thought that the shots came from his own rifle. He'd had Rooney in his sights, hadn't he? He'd been eager to kill Rooney, hadn't he? Well, then the shots must have come from his rifle, mustn't they? All these thoughts tumbled inside his mind in the first few seconds following the loud bark of the rifle.

A rifle, he realized then. Not *his* rifle.

He watched Rooney clutch his chest. He watched Rooney snap his head up to the sky, as if asking why he had been shot. He watched Rooney fall to the ground, still clutching his chest.

And then, bursting from the woods on the other side of the trail, Givens came running like a crazy man, shouting, "Oh, God, Rooney! I thought you was Donlon! Rooney, Rooney, don't you go die on me!"

When he got to Rooney, he threw himself down across the man, apparently knowing that he'd not only wounded him but killed him, and put on a three-minute show of wailing and noisy self-recrimination that even the most theatrical of preachers would have envied.

Only gradually did Jackson realize that Givens was con-

sciously putting on a show. Even in the deepening shadows playing across the path, Givens was glancing around as if to make sure that his audience was still watching. But who was his audience?

Me, Jackson thought. *He's putting an act on for* me.

And then Jackson started laughing so hard, he fell against a tree. He had to pee he was laughing so hard.

He knew now what he'd seen. Givens had hated Rooney almost as much as Jackson did. And so he'd shot him. Now he felt obliged to convince Jackson that this had all been a horrible accident. Who would want to shoot a fine, upstanding man like Rooney?

That was how Givens would shape his defense. And there'd be one other thing, Jackson knew. Givens would ask a certain man—let's say his name was Jackson—to corroborate his story.

Jackson, descending the slope to join Givens and the corpse of Clyde Rooney, still couldn't stop laughing. Hell, yes, he'd corroborate Givens's story! Givens had just done Jackson—and maybe the entire world—a big favor.

A damned big favor.

17

Sheriff Cawthorne usually ate his "widower's meal" over at the café. The steak was good, the waitresses were friendly and he enjoyed being around young families, reminding him of his own youthful days.

But tonight, with no deputy to spell him for supper, he had one of the men from the café bring his meal over. The man also brought Donlon's meal. Tonight it was steak strips with mashed potatoes and gravy. With pumpkin pie as dessert.

He would have enjoyed his meal a whole lot more if he could have taken his mind off what lay ahead for tonight. He'd never been a pessimist. Usually he could find reason for hope in just about any situation. But not this one. Standish was going to create a mob one way or the other. And that mob was going to confront Cawthorne and demand that he hand over Bryce Donlon. Which, of course, he would never do.

He might not be around by dawn. There was a good chance somebody would kill him. And kill Fargo. And, of course, kill young Bryce. He'd heard of towns where the mob was so drunk that they didn't relinquish their grip on the town for forty-eight hours. Just kept guzzling liquor and settling old scores.

He'd prefer death to seeing something like that go on— the complete breakdown of law and order. He'd spent his life trying to make sure that men didn't act like the lowest form of animal.

After he finished his meal, he walked back to the cells. Donlon lay on his bunk, staring at the ceiling.

"I'll be dead by midnight, Sheriff. You probably will be, too."

"I think I can talk some sense into their heads."

"You don't believe that any more than I do."

Cawthorne was silent. He couldn't argue much with what Donlon had said.

"Nobody you can get to help you?" Donlon said. He was strangely calm. He sounded almost resigned to his fate.

"I've been putting out the message ever since Fargo brought you in this morning. You know how it goes. They'd like to help but they can't afford to get crosswise with Standish."

"Good old Standish." Bitterness gave his voice an edge. He no longer sounded resigned. "He never did like me, anyway."

Cawthorne thought over what he was about to say, then said it. "If things get bad tonight, I'm going to give you a Colt." He paused. "You can use it on the mob or on yourself. That'll be up to you."

Donlon sat up instantly. "What the hell're you talking about, use it on myself?"

"In case you did it and you'd rather die by your own hand than swing from a tree."

"But I didn't do it."

"You'd know that better than I do, son. It was just a suggestion."

"Well, I sure as hell don't like it."

"One more thing about the Colt. If I give it to you and you try to shoot me, I'll kill you on the spot. I may be old but I can still take care of somebody like you."

Donlon didn't like being thought of that way. "Somebody like me. What the hell's that supposed to mean?"

"It means you're good at shooting rabbits and tin cans. But you don't have much experience shooting people."

"You pull the trigger, same as always."

"Uh-huh. But rabbits can't shoot back. It's different when you're facing somebody who can kill you. Takes more nerve than shooting at a tin can."

"I can handle myself. You don't have to worry about me."

"I just wanted to give you fair warning. If they should

happen to rush the jail tonight, you and me are on the same side, at least temporarily. Don't try to escape because you wouldn't get ten feet before they got hold of you. The only thing we can do is hunker down here and hope for the best."

Donlon scoffed. " 'Hope for the best.' That's real encouraging."

Cawthorne smiled. "Best I can do, son."

They were a sorry sight.

They straggled into town. No crowd was there to applaud and cheer them. No little kids ran alongside their horses. And the only dog who showed them any interest was an old mutt blind in his left eye who yawned when they passed him.

Eight horses had gone out; eight horses returned. But only seven riders. The eighth, Rooney, had been unceremoniously thrown across a horse. He had the sour smell of death on him. Flies were now his best friends.

Don Jackson rode lead. He still couldn't believe what had happened out there. Givens had killed Rooney for him. He hadn't let Givens in on his secret, of course. Givens drank too much and would likely repeat his tale. All Jackson had told him was that he'd back up his story about confusing Rooney for Bryce Donlon. Very easy to do, he'd say, out there in the trees.

And who'd question either of them except Mrs. Rooney? The deputy hadn't exactly been a beloved figure in this town.

Jackson wasn't much for saloons but as they passed the Golden Garter, the music and the heavy smell of beer and the silver, tinkling laughter of the easy girls made him want to stop and go inside. Have a few beers, say; play several hands of stud poker; and then ride home and tell his wife that Rooney was dead. Just to watch her face. Just to see what kind of emotions she would betray. Did she still love him? Had she ever loved him? Maybe she'd be relieved now that the one person who knew her most shameful secret was dead. Yes, indeed, that would be an interesting moment, watching her face. He had to be careful not to gloat. He had to be real careful.

The other men were silent. The death of Rooney had turned the posse into a wake. Not only hadn't they found Bryce Donlon, they'd brought back their leader thrown across a horse and ready for the undertaker. Posses were supposed to be an escape from the humdrum of dull, everyday life. This one hadn't been anything more than a sham and now a tragedy—at least for the Rooney family, it was a tragedy.

The posse noticed that a small group of men and women stood near the sheriff's office. Right now the group could have been doing nothing more threatening than visiting among themselves. Talking over crop prices or who to support in the next election. This particular group was comprised of merchants and their wives. Not a drunkard or troublemaker or gunfighter in sight.

To the discerning eye this was a devious plot on the part of Theodore Standish. Don't get the rabble-rousers to lead the charge; get the most respectable people you can find. Have them entreat the sheriff to turn Donlon over to them. And that was the correct word, "entreat." Ask reasonably; plead their case on the part of the community. Don't demand; don't threaten. Be good citizens who just want to relieve the town of its burden, the burden being a guilty man sitting uselessly in a cell. A guilty man whose very presence roiled and disturbed the soul of this town.

Yes, a swift, sure feat of justice that would help the town forget the ugly violence that had taken place here and start being its old self again.

And again, these were not troublemakers and rabble-rousers and common drunkards dealing with the sheriff. These were the people who'd helped get him elected again and again—forget that they'd done so at the bidding of Mr. Standish—and these were the people he'd listen to. Or so Theodore Standish hoped, anyway.

Fargo was at the window as they rode up. In the early night gloom, he saw a riderless horse. It took a moment for him to realize that it was Rooney's horse. Then his eyes were able to detail the thing thrown across the animal. Rooney himself.

He opened the door and stepped outside. He brought his Henry with him in case there was trouble waiting for him

in the street. An overeager member of the lynch mob that would soon be forming.

"Bad luck, I'm afraid," Don Jackson said.

Fargo said nothing. He watched as two men carried the corpse to the sidewalk in front of the sheriff's office and laid it down with at least a semblance of care. They stepped quickly away.

By now Cawthorne was standing next to Fargo. He'd brought a lantern. He leaned over, lowering the lantern so that the wound could be seen clearly. To the right of the heart. Two bullets from the looks of things.

"You did this?" Cawthorne said to Jackson.

Givens said, "I did, Sheriff. It was startin' to get dark. We were in some trees. I seen this thing move and I was sure it was Donlon. I shouted for him to stop but he wouldn't and then I took my shots."

"Anybody hear you shout to him?"

Jackson said, "I did. It was loud and clear." He'd never been much of a liar. He hoped his skills had improved some.

"So you're saying it was an accident?"

"It sure was," Jackson said. "A terrible accident."

Givens said, "I feel real bad about this, Sheriff. But I'd appreciate it if you'd be the one who tells his wife. She'd likely get mad at me if I was the one who told her."

With a lynch mob likely to form tonight, Cawthorne knew he didn't have time to worry about this now. From the skeptical look on Fargo's face, Cawthorne could see that Fargo didn't believe the story, either.

"Take him over to the doc's," Cawthorne said. "The rest of you men pack it in for the night."

"You want to talk to me, Sheriff?" Was that a hint of mischief in Givens's voice? That'd be just like him, Cawthorne thought. Not only to kill a man but to gloat over it. Cawthorne wished he had time to deal with this here and now.

But a few minutes later, Fargo and Cawthorne were inside the office, the door bolted. They'd been pouring coffee down their gullets—strong, black, heady coffee—in order to stay alert. They had many hours to go here. Many hours.

"You figure he killed Rooney in cold blood?"

"Yep," Fargo said. "But I'm new here. I don't know what'd make him do it."

"I do," Cawthorne said. Then he told Fargo how Rooney had once run Givens in to jail for disturbing the peace. Givens had never forgiven him, talked about it loudly when pouring them down at the saloon. And had now taken his revenge.

"Soon as we're finished tonight," Cawthorne said, "I'm goin' after him. I didn't like Rooney much but I like murder even less."

Fargo nodded. He was at the window again. He noticed that there were three new faces in the crowd. Coarser faces, meaner faces. These would be the roughnecks working for Standish. These were the men who'd do the initial dirty work. Smash the windows; kick in the door; drag the prisoner out.

Cawthorne stood at the opposite window. "The new ones, they're a tough bunch. Standish imports them whenever he has trouble the local boys aren't tough enough for. They'd kill their own mothers for a gold piece."

Now it was Fargo's turn to go back and see Donlon. The resignation was gone from his face, replaced by fierce worry.

"I can feel that rope around my neck already."

"The sheriff told me to give you a gun if it even gets close to that."

"A gun against a mob ain't gonna be much help."

"You want us to let you go?"

"Damned right. I didn't kill her. I could sneak out now and get away."

"I wouldn't count on it. I'm sure there're a couple of boys on rooftops already. The sheriff just told me that Standish hires gunnies. They know what they're doing. They have front, back and sides covered for sure. They'd shoot you on sight."

Donlon turned back to his cot, threw himself down like a frustrated child. "So I wait here till they drag me out to hang, huh?"

"We're gonna see that doesn't happen."

An angry laugh as he stared at the ceiling. "Oh, sure.

An old man and you. Against a mob. You've got real good odds, Fargo."

There was no talking to him. Fargo couldn't blame him, though. If the mob was up to it, they'd kill Fargo and Cawthorne and then go for Donlon. No matter what Fargo said there was no arguing with that bitter truth.

"I'll talk to you later."

Back up front, Cawthorne said, "I'm giving them another fifteen minutes. Then I'm going out there and try to talk some sense into them."

"You won't talk any sense into those gunnies."

"No. But I'll tell you something. If the decent people out there—if I can convince them to go home and let the law take its course—I think Standish'll pull the gunnies out. He's got to make this look like something the town's in favor of."

"He pretty much runs the town. Why would he worry about what they think of him?"

"Because he has to live here. Because he's never been involved in a killing before. Not as far as I know, anyway. He hires thugs once in a while when somebody tries to cut in on one of his businesses or something like that. But the worst that happens there is that somebody throws a punch or two. This is different. He's putting himself on the line here. And even he can't stand up to a town that won't support him tonight." He offered a sour smile. "This is his big night. Even though Jane's dead, he's got to be careful. He could really overplay his hand tonight."

"There's never been a lynching here?"

"Not in my time. Wouldn't stand for it." He spoke with the pride of a man who respected the law and spent his life honoring it. There were a good number of men like him in the West, even though the Eastern papers continued to promote the idea that most people west of the Mississippi ate all their meals with their hands and relaxed by shooting people in the back.

"How many rifles you have here?"

"You're looking at them, Fargo. Seven of them. Right up there on the rack."

"How about ammunition?"

"Enough to hold off an army for a day or two."

"And nobody else's throwing in with us?"

"Not that I know of."

And that was when the first rock was thrown against the barred window to the right of the front door.

Cawthorne took it in stride. "Startin' a little early. Kinda disappointin'. I figured they'd wait until they were a little drunker."

"The thugs?"

"Nope. Probably locals. The ones you ran into this morning. They were pretty drunk then. Think what they're like now."

Another rock was hurled; it also bounced off the metal bars protecting the windows.

"Have to be a hell of a pitcher to put a rock between those bars," Cawthorne said. "I had them specially made for just that reason. If it ever came to a night like this, I mean."

Fargo leaned in and stared out the window. "Couple torches going now."

"Torches always look pretty at night. At least to me."

"If I didn't know better, I'd say you were enjoying this, Sheriff."

Cawthorne laughed. "Trying to keep my sanity is all. Actually my heart feels like it's gonna tear right through my chest."

Fargo was tensing up, too. No matter how much you planned for a confrontation this size, the reality always overshadowed the planning. Enough rifles, yes; and plenty of ammunition, Cawthorne had said. But five times the number of rifles and three times the amount of ammunition was no substitute for the simple lack of bodies inside the sheriff's office here. The way Fargo figured it, they needed at least six, seven more men to adequately cover front, sides and rear. And even then they'd have to be damned fine shots to hold their own outnumbered this way.

Cawthorne went over to his desk, opened a drawer. Probably get out another pistol, Fargo thought. But no. The lawman took out a bottle of fine sour mash and set it on the desk. "That's for when our spirits wane." Cawthorne smiled. "Had an old army sergeant who always said that.

114

'A little sour mash for when our spirits wane.' Took an arrow right in the forehead, the poor bastard.''

Fargo laughed. "I was worried you were getting sentimental there. Glad you added that business about the arrow in the head. Turned everything right around."

Cawthorne poured himself a healthy drink. "Here's to us," he said, raising his glass in a toast. He grinned. "May God have mercy on our souls."

18

"We'll send him away," Mrs. Tyler Rhodes said. "Parents send their boys away for all sorts of reasons. We'll send him away and nobody will ever suspect."

Tyler sat back in his chair at the dinner table and looked at his wife. She had served him well in every respect— lover, companion, confidante. She had suffered two miscarriages but had continued trying to have a baby even after the doctor had warned her that it was dangerous. She had nursed him through cholera, a gunshot wound and an accident that had kept him in bed for three months. She was a vital part of his business. She charmed the people he worked with—his peer group—and that was important. About other men's wives you heard grumbling. Never about Jenny Rhodes.

He loved her. It was that simple and that complex. He loved her. But if she had a fault, it was the way she had coddled Frank as he'd been growing up. They'd argued about this many times. She'd always promised to let him fend for himself but somehow she always slid back, soon enough, into her old ways. If he got in trouble at school, she blamed the teacher. If he was beaten in a fight, she saw to it that the boy who'd won was punished in some way. And, as in the case where he was caught stealing— stealing! And with all their money!—she claimed to Henry Cawthorne that the boy had suffered from a severe fever and was not himself. Henry, not liking it at all, had gone along only when the tears rolled down her cheeks. Tears worked on Henry much better than bullets.

And now, even after Tyler Rhodes was sure that Bryce

Donlon would be lynched tonight, she made plans for his escape. His unnecessary escape.

"Why send him away? When Bryce dies tonight, the subject will be closed."

"Will it? What if somebody keeps asking questions?"

"Like who? Not Henry. I talked to Standish today. He's going to replace Henry in two weeks. He doesn't have Rooney planted in Henry's office anymore. So now's the time for Henry to go."

"I won't be able to sleep at night if Frank stays here. There's always the possibility that somebody may have seen something—we'll always have that hanging over our heads."

Rhodes wanted to tell her about how he'd taken care of Skunk. Nobody had heard the derringer fire. A few of the ranch hands had probably been curious about Rhodes bringing a wagon to the gazebo but they hadn't said anything. Rhodes drove the wagon to the site of a great gorge. The birds were already picking Skunk's body apart at the bottom of the gorge.

Jenny paced back and forth in the sleek living room with its grand paintings of Paris, its massive Persian rug, its English-manor-house furniture. "I just don't want to wake up someday and find him charged with murder. If we send him away—"

This brought a smile from her husband. "What if he doesn't want to *go* away?"

"Well, he won't have any choice. If we put our foot down—"

"Honey, he's a grown man. A young one, an immature one, but too old for us to order around. If he wants to go away, fine. But I wouldn't count on it. His law practice is just starting to pick up steam and he likes the kind of influence he has because of the family name. If he moves to another town, nobody will know who he is. He'll be just another lawyer. I doubt that he'll like that very well."

She turned to him then. She looked terrified. "I had a dream that they hanged him, Tyler. I saw his eyes bulging out and his feet kicking after they slapped the horse away. Is that what you want for your son?"

And just what was he supposed to say to that?

Mark Jackson said, "Is he going to be in trouble, Pa?"

"I don't think so, son. It was an accident."

The happy family. Ma, Pa, son. That was true of their usual meal, anyway. But not tonight. Ever since Don had told his wife Sarah about Rooney's death, she had started watching him suspiciously—as if a stray expression might reveal to her what had really happened.

"Ma said maybe it *wasn't* an accident."

Jackson was going to pick up his coffee cup just as Mark said that. Now he took his hand from the cup and laid it next to his plate. He didn't seem to notice that it had become a fist. Sarah leaned away, his glare was so angry. "Well, I don't know why she'd say a thing like that, Mark. I was there and saw it. Your ma wasn't. It was getting dark and it was hard to see and Givens thought that he saw Bryce Donlon. He even shouted at him a couple of times to stop where he was. I guess Rooney didn't hear him. Givens was very sorry it happened."

Mark could always sense turmoil in his parents even if he couldn't identify the source. His stomach knotted and a faint sweat slicked his brow. They didn't fight often but when they did he frequently got sick to his stomach. It never got physical but it got so violent verbally that for days after he'd get both headaches and stomachaches. He glanced from his mother to his father. His mother was the hardest to understand. His father had come home with news of Rooney's accidental death. Mark couldn't figure out why this was such an important event to his mother. Had she known Rooney somehow? What was going on here? Were they going to have another one of their fights?

And then his mother did something that shocked him. Usually at this point in an argument her very pretty face got so tight he could see her jaw muscles bunch. And she started launching hateful looks at his father. And saying things designed to make him even madder.

But this time she slumped in her chair and put her hand over her face and began crying. Not great sobs of the sort Mark heard at funerals. But soft, tiny explosions of grief. Her shoulders lurched with each one. Mark was close

enough that he could smell the tears. He'd never realized before that tears *had* a smell.

Then she did something even more surprising. She got up from the table quickly, nearly knocking the bowl of potatoes on the floor as she rose, and hurried to the door. She was outside even before his father could say anything.

His father and Mark sat there.

"This kind of scares me, Pa."

"It'll be all right, son."

"Did she know Mr. Rooney or something?"

Dad said, "She knows Mrs. Rooney. I guess she's just feeling sorry for her. She knows her from church."

"That's right. I see Mrs. Rooney there all the time. But how come Ma doesn't get upset when other men die? You know, Mr. Hasty fell off that horse a couple of months ago and Ma didn't get all sad about that or anything. And she knows Mrs. Hasty from church."

"I guess you just can never tell about women." He stood up. "How about you clear off this table? I'm going to see what your ma is up to."

He found her standing by the rope corral. She'd always found comfort in watching horses. To him they were just utilitarian animals good for work and not much else. But she saw them as some kind of kin who seemed able to read her thoughts.

When he came up to her and tried to slide his arm around her, she said, "You've known all along that Mark was Rooney's boy, haven't you?"

"Yes, I guess I have."

"But you never said anything."

"I loved you too much to say anything. And I loved Mark too much, too." He paused. "But I can see you're still in love with Rooney. The crying and the carrying-on here—"

She raised her face to his and said quietly, "I'm crying for you, Don. For all you've gone through. I'm crying because you're such a decent man. Rooney was something I regretted immediately. I never cared for him much, anyway." Now it was her turn to pause. "I just want you to forgive me—and I'm afraid you won't. That's why I'm crying."

And then Don Jackson felt like crying, too.

Fargo tried the bars on each window in the jail. Short of pulling them out with a rope tied to an animal, there was no way the bars would yield to pressure. The back door was a problem, though. There wasn't time to have it reinforced. Fargo started piling crates and furniture against it until it became a substantial hindrance. They'd have to do a lot of wrestling to get through it. They'd at least be slowed down.

In the office, he took down the rifles one by one, loading them. Cawthorne watched him, sipping his coffee, puffing on a corncob pipe. "I guess you're expectin' the worst, huh?"

Fargo shrugged. "Go down fighting, if nothing else."

"I still think I can talk some sense into them."

"You looked outside in the last ten minutes?"

"Bigger crowd?"

"About double the size."

Cawthorne pushed himself up from the chair. He had noisy old-man bones. "Guess I should go out there."

"I'd advise against it."

"You in charge now, Fargo?" He said it funny but it came off sharp.

"Free advice."

"And you know what that's worth."

Cawthorne had his pride, Fargo thought. He didn't intend to take orders from some upstart drifter. "I'd appreciate you covering me from one of the windows."

"Will do."

Then: "I got to do this, Fargo. Show my face, I mean. Show I ain't scared. If they think I'm scared, it's gonna just get worse."

"Like you say, Sheriff, it's your call."

"Sorry I snapped at you."

Fargo smiled. "I think I'll probably get over it."

Just as Cawthorne started toward the door, he bumped his knee against the edge of his desk. In that moment, Fargo saw how old and weak the lawman really was. Cawthorne touched his hand to his knee and slumped back into his chair. The eyes he showed Fargo were those of a

youngster who didn't understand why such great pain had been inflicted on him.

"I just need a minute here."

"You want me to go out there instead?"

Fargo instantly regretted his words. He saw that he'd wounded the old man far worse than the sharp edge of the desk had.

"You don't think I got it in me?"

"I know you got it in you, Sheriff."

"You're a liar. You think I'll go out there and they won't listen to me because I'm so old."

"Now you're putting words in my mouth."

"Words you'd say yourself if you had any guts."

Fargo shrugged. "I figure you know what you're capable of and what you're not capable of. If you want to go out there, go ahead."

"You're damned right I'll go. And when I come back in, you'll see just how wrong you were about me."

"I'm sorry I said anything."

"And I don't want your pity." As he said this he brought a large fist down so hard on the desk that everything on top danced and toppled. "So maybe it's better if you just shut up."

Fargo nodded.

This time when he approached the door, Cawthorne did so with a limp. Fargo tried not to notice, kept vigil at the window.

Cawthorne looked as if he might say something else, but then thought the better of it. He took his hat from the hook by the door. He tucked in his shirt, made sure his holster and gun were in the proper position and then took his handkerchief and dusted off his badge. It rode high and prominent on the front of his work shirt.

Fargo said, "I could at least go with you."

"Remember what I said about you shutting up?"

Fargo nodded. Shrugged.

"I'll be back. You just stay at that window."

Fargo didn't say anything.

Cawthorne opened the door. The crowd noise tripled instantly. People were shouting and pointing. Cawthorne's

sudden appearance was like a famous person walking onto a stage. A famous, *controversial* person. Some applauded and cheered; others booed.

Fargo had a bad feeling about it all.

The lawman sensed that these weren't the people he'd known and served all these years. Oh, they looked the same and their voices sounded the same. But there was something different about them that could only be attributed to the fact that they were no longer individuals but part of a living, growing organism called a mob. Otherwise temperate, sensible people had handed over their will, their brains and their fate to the collective beast that now occupied a large portion of the otherwise empty street.

Not a smile, not a greeting, not a hospitable gaze on the masks they now wore. They were strangers to him now.

The liquor didn't help matters. He figured that more than half the crowd was drunk and that included many of the women. His eyes lifted to the rooftops of the buildings across from him. A pair of men with rifles watched him.

The crowd was noisy but nobody was saying anything he could make much sense of. He raised his hand. He was surprised that they complied so quickly with his order to be quiet.

"I know why you're here. And I don't blame you. A terrible murder was committed in our little town the other night and it's hard to think about anything else until it's resolved. I think we've got the man who killed Jane Standish in jail. You'll notice I said 'I think.' Because right now that's the best answer I can give anybody who asks me. But I'm not a mind reader and I'm not God. So I can't be positive that Bryce Donlon killed her.

"That's why I'm asking you to give me a little time here. Donlon isn't going anywhere. He's locked up good and tight. But I want a few days to ask around, to make sure that he's our man. That's how it has to be if he's gonna get a fair trial. And I aim to see that he gets exactly that.

"A lot of you would rather be home. But Mr. Standish ordered you to come down here. I don't have anything against Mr. Standish. And I understand why he wants to get his hands on Donlon. But we all have to be careful here tonight. Things could get away from us. Things could

end up worse than they are right now. So what I'm asking you is to turn around and go back to your homes and let the law take its course. Don't do something foolish that we'll all regret tomorrow morning."

This was when the three gunnies stepped forward. Moments after, they were joined by Givens. The gunnies stood right in front of the sheriff, a line of grizzled men eager for trouble. They were getting paid by Standish to make trouble. Givens made a fourth. He was doing it because he hated everything and everybody associated with this jail. He felt he'd suffered a great indignity by spending even a single night in a cell here.

"That goes for you men, too. Givens, I know how much you hate being in jail. But that's where you're going to end up again tonight if you're not careful. And the same goes with you other three. I'm not going to put up with any kind of shenanigans."

But he could see by the sneers and smirks on their faces that his words were wasted. He'd apparently just given them even more reason to see him as a doddering old lawman whose prime years were long past.

He recognized only one of them, a man named Lynott. Lynott, a thickset man with heavy features and a knife-sharp smirk, said, "I'm gonna start walking toward you, Sheriff. If you're smart you'll give me the keys and then get out of my way. Nobody expects you to die for Donlon. So you just go along with what we want to do and you'll be able to get a good night's sleep. Otherwise you might wind up in the graveyard."

The crowd was getting what it had come to see. These three gunnies were going to go over or around Cawthorne—whatever it took. They were going to haul Donlon out here for all to see, for all to judge, and then they were going to find an accommodating tree and hang him.

Fargo knew he had to move now. He left his Henry behind. He stood on the sidewalk and said, "I don't like those numbers. Four against one."

Cawthorne said, "You stay inside. I can handle this."

Givens laughed. "I told you I'd get even with you for putting me in that jail of yours, Cawthorne. Looks like the time has come."

Cawthorne was slow to react. By the time he'd swung his rifle in Givens's direction, Givens had slicked his gun from its holster and was ready to fire on the old lawman. But he hadn't counted on Fargo. Orange flame exploded from Fargo's Colt. There was a roar as one of the other three gunnies drew down on Fargo in the same instant.

But Fargo was so fast he had time to kill Givens and then throw himself to the ground, where the gunny fired uselessly, trying to hit the man who was rolling along the sidewalk. He was so intent on killing Fargo that he left himself open for the Trailsman to fire back at him. Fargo had much better luck than the gunny had. Fargo's bullets split his forehead into two pieces.

The other two gunnies were now disinclined to get involved in the shoot-out.

The dusty street. The full moon. The shadows playing on the false fronts. The player piano music from two different saloons. The smells of road apples, sweat, liquor, malt from beer, cigarette smoke, cigar smoke, pipe smoke.

This was the scene as everybody present seemed frozen in place, gunfire still echoing, clouds of gun smoke shimmering as it began to disintegrate on the night air.

Fargo was on his feet again. He strode over to the two gunnies and took their Colts. Then he marched them into jail and straight into a cell. They knew better than to say anything. Fargo was in a killing mood.

"Standish'll get us out of here right soon," said one of the gunnies from the cell.

"We'll see," Fargo said.

"You got the upper hand now," the other one said. "But not for long."

"Thanks for the warning."

Standish might have a lot of money but apparently the supply of hired guns in this area wasn't the best. Fargo was sure that Standish hadn't meant for his three hires to actually shoot anybody. They were only supposed to stir up trouble and keep it at a boil. The theory being that Cawthorne, faced with a mob that wanted Bryce Donlon, would give in without a fight and let them have him. Important as Standish was, not even he could get involved in the cold-blooded murder of a lawman. But these three couldn't con-

trol themselves. Their natural instinct was to kill people. And if Fargo hadn't come outside to help Cawthorne, the old lawman would be dead by now.

Fargo was two steps from the front door when somebody shouted, "Grab him!"

Fargo's first thought was that somebody was coming after Cawthorne. Fargo stepped through the door. It took him a moment to recognize what was going on. The crowd had dispersed into small knots up and down the long street. About a dozen people remained in front of the sheriff's office. And it was four men from this number that were now clutching Cawthorne.

But they weren't trying to hurt him. They were trying to help him.

"Heart attack!" one of the men shouted to Fargo. Then, louder: "Somebody run and get the doc."

19

"I suppose it was all the excitement," Doc Renard said, the tip of his white goatee bobbing as he spoke. He was a pear-shaped man in a derby with a fancy walking stick he'd seemed reluctant to set down. "I kept tellin' the bastard he should retire. But what the hell do I know? I'm just his doc."

This was an hour after the shoot-out in the street. Everybody had gone home or gone to saloons. Standish certainly hadn't gotten his money's worth. He hadn't counted on the town's affection for Cawthorne.

Right now the lawman was a light gray in color. He came in and out of sleep violently, as if escaping nightmares. Doc Renard had him laid out on the table in the jail's spare room. He'd joked that he'd had almost as many patients here as in his own office.

Fargo had the front door locked. He hadn't moved anything from the back door. It was still piled high with obstacles for intruders. Right now he was the one and only lawman in town.

Doc Renard nodded for them to leave the room. He turned down the lamp, took a final check of Cawthorne's pulse at the wrist and then followed Fargo out.

They didn't talk until they were up front. Fargo poured them each a tin cup of coffee. "He going to make it?"

"Hard to say. I ain't much for predictions, anyway. Need another six, seven hours to see how he goes before I'd even venture a guess."

"I wish you could stay here tonight."

"Not much I can do about that, Fargo. I got two mid-wives who told me their ladies are ready to give birth. That's enough to keep two docs busy, let alone one."

"If they're midwives, why do they need you?"

Doc Renard scowled. "They both had problems the last year. A pair of twins died on one of them and the other one lost a mother. They just want me to check in and see how things're goin'. You lose a couple like that, you get spooked. Natural reaction, I guess."

The doctor picked up his Gladstone bag and said, "Both these ladies are in town here. So it won't be hard to get to me. If you need me, send a runner."

Fargo smiled sourly. "And where do I get a runner? I'm the whole show here tonight, in case you haven't noticed."

Doc Renard laughed. "This is your night to shine, Fargo. You handle everything real good tonight, they'll probably name a street after you or something." Then he winked at Fargo. "Sorry all this came down on your shoulders, Fargo. I guess things just happen that way sometimes."

He walked over to the door, began unlocking both the key lock and the bolt lock. When he got it open, a man stood there with a repeater rifle. "What the hell you doin' here, Jackson?" Doc Renard said. "If I had a wife as pretty as yours, I'd be home in bed with her."

"I want to talk to Fargo."

"You going to shoot him with that rifle, are you?" The doctor had a way of joshing people that walked a fine line between humor and seriousness. Sometimes it was difficult to tell which was which.

"Not hardly. I want to tell him I'll be his deputy."

Doc Renard opened the door wide so Fargo could see. "You hear that, Fargo? Jackson here is volunteering to be your deputy."

Jackson looked all right to Fargo but that didn't mean a damned thing. "He a good man, Doc?"

"Yep. Don't drink much, don't cuss in front of ladies and has been known to take a bath at least twice a week. And you should see that wife of his."

Jackson had smiled about everything Doc Renard had said—right up to the mention of his wife. A frown had taken

over the smile. Renard saw what his words had wrought. He tapped Jackson on the arm and said, "Just kiddin', son. You should be complimented I talk about her so much."

Jackson grinned. "Yeah, I guess so."

Doc Renard said, "Fargo, you need to check on him every fifteen minutes. We made him a comfortable bed back there and he'll probably sleep. But if you hear him start to wake up, you hightail it back there pronto."

With that he was gone, leaving Fargo with a man who was mysteriously volunteering to be his deputy.

Theodore Standish sat on his screened-in porch with his cigar and scotch and soda. Twenty minutes ago he'd heard the gunfire from the center of town. At first he'd been encouraged, assuming that his wishes—the wishes he'd paid for—had been carried out. By now, he'd hoped, Bryce Donlon was in the process of being hanged.

But two minutes ago he'd learned differently when one of his own men rode hard back to the mansion and told him what had actually transpired. The man named Fargo had killed one of his gunnies and Givens. Cawthorne had had a heart attack. And now, the crowd had dispersed and Fargo was in charge.

All men have disappointments. Even the richest and most powerful. But Standish had disappointments so seldom that when one came his way he never knew quite how to deal with it. For a time it always immobilized him. He would sit and ponder how it was possible in this very knowable Theodore Standish universe—that Theodore Standish could possibly have been let down.

He was at that point now. He had given the maid orders that no one, including Mrs. Standish, was to bother him under any conditions whatsoever. He wanted to be completely alone on this second-floor porch, alone with the fireflies and the stars and the ragged silhouette of mountains against the velvety dark sky.

He wasn't much of a drinker so he hadn't had to shout out an order for a drink freshener in more than a half hour. But he loved his cigars and he tormented the soft night air with the stench and the greasy gray look of the smoke.

And tonight it was his cigar that showed him the thing

he must do now. He had just scratched a wooden match against the sole of his boot when the flame caught his eye and a picture formed instantly in his mind.

He bellowed so loudly for the maid that the night birds stuttered in their song. As ruler of the universe, he had the right to interrupt the natural flow of things, didn't he?

"The bunkhouse. Steve Adair. Bring him."

"Yessir," the young maid said. The man terrified her under the most tranquil of circumstances. When he was this upset she found it difficult to swallow, to draw breath. She stumbled on her way out. Humiliated, she gathered herself and rushed to the vestibule. . . .

. . . leaving Standish with his thoughts of his daughter. Friends said that the only thing Ted Standish hadn't managed to corrupt in his life was his daughter, Jane. He had long ago turned his simple but sweet wife into nothing more than an aging doll who accompanied him when wives were required. But Jane . . . Jane resented his money, his power, his selfishness. She even tried the most impossible task ever attempted by a human being—she attempted to change her father. And to his great secret pride, she'd done so to at least a small degree. She got him to give considerable money to charities; to improve the pay and the working conditions of the people who worked in his various enterprises; and she even got him to rely less on his thugs and more on the democratic process where town politics were concerned.

He smiled when he thought of these things. He really had been proud of her, though he could never admit it to her. Hell, he could barely admit it to himself. Of all the people who'd tried to intimidate, pressure, bully and coerce Theodore Martin Standish into doing something he didn't want to do . . . only one had ever been able to do it . . . a slip of a girl with dancing, dark eyes and the sweet face of a slightly mischievous angel . . . his beloved daughter, Jane.

And there was no doubt who'd killed her.

And there was no doubt that his first attempt tonight to get satisfaction had failed. Had failed not only him. But had failed the memory of Jane, as well.

And there was no doubt that this night was not over.

Oh, no, for Theodore Standish, this night had just begun.

*   *   *

"Where are you going?" Mrs. Tyler Rhodes said.

"Isn't that kind of a foolish question to ask?" Rhodes snapped. He had just changed from a suit into the range clothes he liked to wear. He had also strapped on a holster and a .45. She hadn't seen him wear a gun in years.

She sat in a Queen Anne chair next to a screened window. The heat was dissipating quickly now and she meant to enjoy it. "I think you owe me an apology for that remark."

Rhodes nodded. "I do at that, dear. It's just—"

"It's just that it all fell through tonight."

"Yes."

"Bryce Donlon's still alive, meaning that our son could still be found guilty."

"If only he could remember what the hell happened."

"You were here. You saw him. He was lucky to know his name. I don't think I've ever seen anybody that drunk."

"I wonder what he's doing now. I stopped by his office this afternoon and he wouldn't see me. The Swinnerton woman said he was too busy."

She turned in the chair so she could get a better look at him. "Did something happen to you this afternoon?"

Too quickly, he said, "No. Why?"

"Well, you're biting your fingernails, which you haven't done in a long time. And you were so distracted at dinner I couldn't get your attention without practically shouting at you."

"Just worried about our boy. It's only natural."

But disbelief showed in her gaze. She wondered if this was "the truth, the whole truth and nothing but the truth," as their son Frank liked to joke at the dinner table when his father told a story that stretched credibility. With some wine in him, Tyler Rhodes could tell some whoppers. He could also keep things from her. He was one of those men who believed that a wife should learn about some things and be kept from others. This was based on the belief that men were stronger than women, though she knew better. You couldn't generalize. Some men were stronger than some women and vice versa. But there was no convincing Tyler of that.

"So you're sure that nothing happened to you this afternoon that I should know about?"

"I don't keep things from you. You know that."

"There's another one of your whoppers, Tyler. You keep things from me all the time."

"Not important things."

"Yes, but you decide what's important and what's not important."

He shook his head. "This isn't the time for that discussion."

"Do I at least get to know where you're going?"

"I'm riding over to see Standish. See what he's thinking of right now."

She sat up straight in her chair. "You think there's still something that can be done?"

"Of course. Our son's life is at stake here. You don't think I'd give up that easily, do you?"

"I was afraid—" She stopped herself. "You seemed so quiet after we heard that Henry Cawthorne had a heart attack and that the crowd broke up. I just thought you'd given up."

"Well, our son won't leave town. And he has no defense for himself if he's ever asked where he was that night—somebody's got to take care of him. And that's me."

"Us. Not just you. Both his parents. Us."

He knew he'd made the sort of mistake that cut her. The worst thing was that the cut had been accidental. He didn't mind hurting people's feelings on purpose. You made a calculation to do it and you did it. But when you hurt people inadvertently—that was one of the worst social sins to Rhodes. Because they never quite forgave you, never quite believed that the insult had been unintentional.

"I'm going now, dear."

"Be careful."

"Say prayers."

Usually she responded effusively when he requested God's intervention but now she hesitated. "I don't know if it's right to ask for help with this. We're deceiving people."

"Yes," he said, "but we're saving our son. Isn't that more important than anything else?"

20

"But I *wanted* to kill him. I went there to kill him."

"But you didn't kill him. Givens killed him."

"But I would have if Givens—"

Fargo had taken on a new role tonight. Not only was he acting sheriff—at least until somebody came in and officially removed him—he was now acting as father confessor to a distraught man named Don Jackson, who also happened to be Fargo's one and only volunteer deputy.

"I might have killed him, Fargo."

"But you didn't. And from what you tell me, you love the boy like he's your own."

"Yes, I do."

"And you seem willing to forgive your wife. And you say she loves you—Well, every once in a while things turn out all right. At least in my experience."

Jackson leaned his heavyset body back in the creaking chair that belonged to the smallest desk. "Maybe you're right. I guess there are signs."

"What kinda signs?"

"Well, we still make love."

"That's a good sign."

"And she still kisses me a lot and tells me she loves me."

"That's another good sign."

"And she never forgets my birthday. Always makes a fuss. And a big chocolate cake."

"One more good sign."

"Then maybe—"

Fargo didn't smile. He didn't want to let on that he knew what was going on here. Jackson was talking himself into

a positive frame of mind and Fargo was aiding and abetting by responding enthusiastically to each proof of the wife's love.

"You made me feel a lot better, Fargo. When I heard that nobody would throw in with you—I'm glad I came down here."

"I'm glad you came down here, too. I'm in need of an extra gun. Actually, I could use three or four."

"You don't think it's over yet?"

"Not hardly. Men with the kind of money and power that Standish has don't give up that easy."

"I feel sorry for him. Jane was a real sweet girl."

"I feel sorry for him up to the point where he thinks he's the voice of law and order. You can't buy that, not even with all his money. And like I said, it's not over yet. The night's still pretty young."

Fargo walked over to the rack of rifles. "These are loaded and ready to go. I don't know what they'll try next but we have to be ready for anything. We've got plenty of ammunition to get us through the night. If they decide to rush us."

"What else would they do?"

Fargo frowned. "That's something only Mr. Standish knows. And I'm sure he's working on it right now."

Jackson was about to say something when somebody knocked on the front door. Both men went into action. Guns were drawn, aimed at the door.

"Who is it?" Fargo said.

"Grace. Grace Donlon."

"You alone, Grace?"

"Yes. I want to see my brother."

Fargo stepped to the window. Pulled back the drape. Scanned the street. He looked for sight of anybody who might have forced Grace to come up to the door. Get Fargo to open up for her—and then come in right behind her. But she appeared to be telling the truth. She appeared to be alone.

"Cover me," Fargo said and went to the door.

The sweet, seductive scent of perfume wasn't an aroma he'd planned on encountering on a night like this. Instead of incipient violence and a town all stirred up, her perfume

spoke of slow and pleasant seduction, of the safety and serenity of a woman's boudoir. Of pleasures of mind and spirit that were the opposite of gun battles and carnage.

The red-haired Grace was fetching as always. In her white cotton blouse and black butternuts, her body was, like her perfume, a reminder of better moments in human endeavors. Nothing tawdry like sweating through a night trying to stop a mob from lynching a prisoner. Only her troubled but still regal face reminded Fargo of why she was here. She was afraid for her brother's life. Very simple.

"I just wanted to see Bryce."

"I notice you're wearing a gun."

She tapped the handle of the Colt riding in her holster. "My father taught us both to shoot before we were seven years old. I can hold my own, believe me. And the way this night is going I thought I'd better bring some protection."

Fargo nodded.

"Evening, Don," she said.

Jackson nodded. "Howdy, Grace."

"He's all right, if that's what you're worried about," Fargo said as he led Grace back to the cells.

"What if the mob would've gotten in here?"

"I already discussed that with him," Fargo said as they continued walking to the back of the place. "I would've given him a gun. It'd be up to him what he wanted to do with it."

"He's a troublemaker, not a killer. I can't imagine him shooting anybody he knows. He grew up with all these people."

"Some men use it on themselves," Fargo said.

"The guilty ones," she snapped. "But Bryce isn't guilty."

Donlon must have heard them coming. He stood at the cell door, straining to watch as they approached him.

"Your sister would like to see you," Fargo said. Then, before she could offer any protest, Fargo snatched the gun from her holster.

She looked shocked and angry.

"Sorry, Grace. It'd be too tempting for Bryce. He'd have himself a gun and he'd most likely turn it on me so he could get out of here."

"I told you," she said coldly. "He isn't a killer."

"He wouldn't have to kill me. He could just knock me out with it and be gone before I came to."

Then, again before she could protest, he patted her down quickly.

"Skye, this is ridiculous. I'm not the enemy."

"I know you're not. But I have to do my job and that means checking anybody I put in the cell with a prisoner."

"Even an innocent one?" she said gently, her enormous eyes reflecting hurt now.

His own voice softened, too. "Yes, even innocent ones."

He eased the key in the cell door and turned it hard to the right. He pulled the door open and stepped back, letting her walk inside. Then he locked the two of them in together.

"Take all the time you want," Fargo said. "Just holler out when you're ready to go."

"I appreciate this," Grace said.

"My pleasure," Fargo said. "Remember, just holler out."

"But we only have three men," Tyler Rhodes said.

"We won't need more than that."

Rhodes was instantly reminded about why he was always uncomfortable around Theodore Standish. Because Standish always talked to him as if he were a particularly dense six-year-old. Even when he was enraged over his daughter's murder, he found it within himself to scoff at Rhodes. "What did you think, Tyler? That we'd need an army? You need to use your head and think things through."

This was Standish's way of reminding Rhodes that Standish was richer, more powerful and superior in every way that mattered. And probably in a number of ways that didn't—for the record he was better at croquet and pinochle, and he had a greater mental library of dirty jokes.

A Negro butler appeared with a bottle of good bourbon and two glasses. The screened-in porch was chilly now in the night. Given what the men were planning, the birdsong that traveled the air seemed absurdly sweet and innocent. But these were determined men. Standish wanted vengeance for his daughter. Rhodes wanted protection for his son.

The butler vanished into the shadows of the house, leaving the men to taste the liquor that had been brought them.

Rhodes said, "We have to be careful that nobody gets hurt except Donlon."

Standish snapped: "You think I give a damn about that? After what happened to my little Jane? I don't care who gets hurt or who doesn't. I just want the sonofabitch dead."

Rhodes was going to argue but then he had a terrible realization. He'd always thought of himself as a decent man. He'd told himself that he would have been just as successful as Standish if only he'd been as ruthless. But now he realized that that wasn't true. Look what he was about to do. Look at how calmly he'd set about doing it. Look at how quickly he was acquiescing to Standish's words—*I don't care who gets hurt or who doesn't.* It's a terrible thing for a man to realize that he's not as decent as he's always thought. That when you come right down to it, he's just as ruthless as the most ruthless man in the territory.

"That's the way it has to be, Ty."

"I agree."

"Good. I thought you were going to back out for a minute there."

"I want him dead, too, Ted."

And then Standish said: "That's what makes me curious about you, Ty."

This was the part he'd dreaded. The inevitable question. Ted Standish was too shrewd not to think it, not to ask it. "Why're you so eager to help me with this?"

"Because I know what your daughter meant to you."

"You don't even like me, Ty." His tone of voice indicated that he was having some mean fun at Rhodes's expense.

"Why, that's not true. I—"

"In fact, you resent me. In fact, every time we've worked together, I've come out a little better than you on the deal. You have to resent me for that. But here you are offering to help me break the law like this. Makes me wonder just what's going on here."

"I know what Jane meant to you."

Standish's laugh was sharp, arrogant. "You're going to

stick to that, huh? You're going to be my friend even though you don't like me—even though you probably *hate* me, in fact—and even though you don't think we have enough men for the job."

"I don't know why you're saying all this, Ted."

"Because you're lying. You know you're lying and I know you're lying, Ty. You're here for your own reason and I want to figure out what that is." Then he reached across the small wicker table separating them from each other and placed his hand on Rhodes's shoulder. "But you know what, Ty?" And his voice was kinder than Rhodes had ever heard it. "Right now I don't give a damn *why* you're here. I just want to tell you that I'm grateful you showed up to help me."

If Rhodes didn't know better, he'd have thought that Ted Standish was about to cry.

She looked so clean, so fresh, so . . . new. She might have been one of those miracle nurses in the romances she read. So wholesome, purposeful. Able to save people from the worst of predicaments.

Bryce Donlon and his sister, Grace, hadn't always agreed. Big sister and little brother had had all the usual arguments, especially after their folks had died. She'd tried to keep him out of trouble, something—he now admitted— it would have taken a small army to do. But now she reminded him of all the good things he'd had in life—and spurned. A loving home life, more education if he'd wanted it, and the opportunity for several different good jobs. But he had wasted it all on fights, tantrums, obsessions, especially when it had come to Jane Standish. . . . He'd cast it all aside just to have his own way. And it hadn't mattered whether it was a big issue or a small one. He'd wanted his way and gotten it.

And for all it had been worth . . . he'd ended up here, huddling in a dingy cell, afraid that he was about to be dragged to his death by hanging.

If only his sister really were the nurse of those romance novels . . . if only she really could save him.

"I'm just glad our folks aren't alive to see this, Grace."

"Right now the only person I'm worried about is you."

"Fargo says he can protect me."

"He means well. I like him and respect him. But Standish—he won't even give you a chance to speak for yourself. To give your side of the story. Everybody tells me that he's been all over town today telling people that you killed Jane and that you need to be punished for it right away."

Donlon sat on the edge of his cot, running his hands through his hair. Even with the drop in temperature, he was sweaty. Nerves. Fear. Desperation.

"He scattered the mob before," Donlon said.

"I know. He's a tough man."

He glanced at his sister. "You sound as scared as I do."

She went over and sat next to him on the cot. Slid her arm around him. Held him close as she had done when he was still a boy. "I know you're going to be all right. I have faith in Fargo."

"You didn't sound like it."

"I— Everybody gets frightened once in a while. I guess it was seeing you in this cell. You look so young and—vulnerable, Bryce. That's all it was. Just seeing you like that." She kissed him on the cheek. "You should try and get some sleep."

Everything was tumbling together. Words, phrases, thoughts. He'd apparently misunderstood Grace. She'd sounded as if Fargo couldn't hold off whatever threat Standish was about to make. But now she sounded just the opposite—no cause for alarm—Fargo could handle all this with no problem.

He was so fatigued from anxiety, from outright terror. Just picturing what a torch-bearing mob could do to him if they decided to make a run on the sheriff's office . . . My God!

And that was when he couldn't handle it any longer—not any of it—that was when he put his face into his sister's shoulder and began to weep. She held him tight. And soon enough, she was weeping, too.

21

The three men started at the back of the sheriff's office. They each carried buckets of highly flammable oil that they splashed all over the wooden structure. This was quickly followed by setting the fire and standing back momentarily to admire what they'd just done. Even they were surprised at how quickly the flames climbed up into the dark desert sky. Even they were surprised at how hungrily those flames spread to the roof of the one-story building. Even they were surprised at how eagerly the flames began to collapse the roof.

Fargo said, "Smoke."

"Yeah," Jackson said.

And that was when they heard Bryce Donlon cry out. His sister had left five minutes ago. He was back there and so were the gunnies.

Fargo rushed to the door separating the front from the back of the building. The instant he opened the door, thick gray smoke—ghostlike—roiled toward him, gagging him on the spot. The fire had already consumed much of the back half of the place.

As he tried to rush into the center of the blinding smoke, he heard Jackson shout behind him: "I can hear the roof caving in, Fargo! Don't go back there!"

As Fargo plunged ahead, a part of him dealt angrily with the truth of what was going on here. Standish had failed to incite a riot so now he'd turned to destroying Bryce Donlon with fire. Oh, not Standish personally. Men like Standish never did their own underhanded work. This would have been done by a couple of his hired thugs. They would have

used oils that burned quickly. Arson was hardly unknown in the West. Just ask insurance companies. Hired criminals now numbered arson among their standard talents.

For the first time Fargo felt the boiling heat of the flames themselves. He waded through the smoke, working toward the sound of the cries. But the closer he got the heat became so intense that parts of his face literally felt as if they would melt away. Jackson was still shouting for him to come back to the front of the building. Jackson didn't seem to realize that within a few minutes there would *be* no front of the building. It would be flame, smoke and ash just like the back of the building.

The crash made Fargo jump. He was momentarily confused—the smoke was starting to make him dizzy, nauseous—but then he realized that it was the roof at the back of the building. Pieces of it had started breaking up, collapsing.

"Fargo! Help me! Help me!"

Somewhere in the murk Bryce Donlon stood trapped in his cell. Fargo had to get to him. Innocent or guilty, he didn't deserve to die this way. Fargo had to free him, if only to stand trial and be found culpable in the murder of Jane Standish.

"Fargo! Please! Please help me!"

Each cry became more frantic, more desperate.

The two gunnies in the other cell also began shouting. And then Fargo remembered that Cawthorne was resting in the spare room.

Fargo pictured himself reaching the cells. Taking his keys and opening the doors. Freeing them all from their flaming prison.

Only then did he realize that he should have found the cells by now. Only then did he realize that he was lost in the smoke. Only then did he realize that his breath was coming in gasps now, that his sense of direction was gone completely, that he felt as if he was about to pass out.

Oddly, the cries seemed to recede. As if they were miles away.

Fargo began staggering. He raised his hand, trying to push away smoke. His eyes stung, his stomach heaved.

And then he was—falling.

He did so with great disbelief. Fargo didn't like to admit that he wasn't able to finish an important job. He'd come back here to rescue Bryce Donlon and the others and, dammit, he was going to do it.

But he knew suddenly that he *wasn't* going to do it.

He knew suddenly that the cries and screams he heard now weren't the cries and screams of men begging for rescue. . . . Rather, they were the sounds men make at the moment they're dying.

These were Fargo's thoughts as he began falling through the smoke, falling without any possibility of rescue himself, falling so hard that when his forehead struck the floor, he was unconscious instantly.

Instantly.

22

Coughing so hard he thought he would throw up. A headache that felt as if his skull had been cleaved in half. A general physical malaise a lot like flu.

And where the hell was he exactly?

Slatted wood beneath him. He could feel the separations against his back. A chilly wind. His hair mussed, his nose very cold. And voices. Only one of them familiar. Don Jackson.

He sat up. He wasn't sure he had the strength to make it but he decided that thinking about it, weighing the odds, was a waste of time. Better to just try it. And he succeeded.

Main Street. Everything stark shadows in the moonlight. A few horses hitched to posts. Muted player piano music from one of the saloons, as if they were playing it against town rules or something. And then the overpowering stench of the fire and his first look at the eight men who'd formed the fire brigade. The stench was a mixture of burned wood, scorched roofing and the water used to dampen the fire. But the brigade would be at it all night. They'd managed to contain the fire, stop it from spreading, but it was still active in spots.

"He's awake!" somebody shouted.

He didn't bother to find out whose voice it was. Realizing that he'd been laid out here on the sidewalk, a blanket thrown over him, he began to remember what had happened. It didn't take long to remember that young Bryce Donlon had been trapped in the back of the sheriff's office.

Don Jackson helped him to his feet. He was so dizzy, he felt as if he'd pitch forward. Jackson steadied him.

Then Grace was there. Her voice was plaintive, tearful. "At least *you're* alive, Skye."

Even in his slightly confused state, Fargo didn't have to ask what that meant. Bryce Donlon had died in the fire.

Jackson pushed a pint bottle of rye at him. "Doc said to give you this when you came to. He had two emergencies in his office so we had to put you out on the sidewalk. He said that he thinks Cawthorne is going to make it. He seems to be coming around."

"Who pulled me out?"

Grace said, "Don did. He also tried to get to Bryce and the gunnies, the same as you did. But he couldn't."

"Thanks," Fargo said to Jackson. Then: "I need some coffee and a little bit more of that rye and then I'm going after Standish."

"No, Skye! He'll have you killed."

"Then he'll be shooting a duly sworn lawman. He's already going to prison for killing Bryce. Killing a lawman just might get him hanged."

Jackson said, "You won't have to go far. He's right up the street at the Golden Garter. He and Rhodes both. Far as I can figure they were in this together."

Fargo, his mind clearing finally, said, "That make any sense to you? Why would Rhodes get involved in this?"

"I don't know, Skye. But they're together, which you don't see very often. And they're sitting in a saloon, which you see even less."

Grace took Fargo's arm. "My brother's dead, Skye. I don't want to see you die, too."

"That'll be up to Standish."

"Talk him out of it, Don. Please."

"She may have a point, Skye. Standish runs this town. And with Rhodes with him, nobody else has the power to even question what he does. You say he's going to prison but I doubt it. Not with his connections. He'll find a way out of this. He always does." He paused. "And that includes killing a duly sworn lawman, Skye. He'll get out of that, too, if he needs to. How about thinking it over for a while?"

Fargo looked up the street to the Golden Garter.

"There," he said, "I've thought it over. I'm going."

And with that, he set off.

* * *

By the time Fargo reached the saloon, Don Jackson had fallen into step with him. Jackson carried a sawed-off shotgun. "Looks like we may need it." Jackson nodded to the two rifle-armed men who stood sentry on the steps of the Golden Garter.

As the pair drew nearer, the guards pointed their rifles in the general direction of the approaching men.

Fargo spoke up. "I'm the acting sheriff and I want to go inside."

"Mr. Standish said we wasn't supposed to let you in."

The faces of the men were lost in the shadows created by the overhang of the saloon. Only their eyes could be seen clearly in the gloom beneath the brims of their hats—feral, cold eyes.

"Mr. Standish isn't the law. I am. I'm acting on behalf of Sheriff Cawthorne."

One of the men snorted. "If you're tryin' to impress us, you sure ain't gonna do it by hookin' up with Cawthorne."

Fargo put his right boot on the first step of the five leading up to the saloon. "I'm going in there."

"Then you're goin' in with a chestful of lead, mister."

Fargo noticed how quiet it was for a saloon. No music. No laughter. Not even much in the way of hushed voices conversing. He could feel the tension. They'd been expecting him for some kind of showdown.

"This is my last warning," Fargo said.

"His last warning," one man said to the other.

"You're crazy, mister. We got two rifles on you."

"I can see that. But Jackson there's got a sawed-off. You'll be able to kill me but Jackson'll have time to cut one of you in half."

"And I'll be lookin' forward to it," Jackson said.

"You got it wrong, mister. I can shoot you and Verne here can shoot Jackson."

And that was when Fargo, feeling that the two guards had been sufficiently lulled into conversation, threw himself upward, diving low enough to seize the guard on the left around the knees and bring him down. The man's rifle boomed in the quiet night. The other guard instinctively turned to help him. That was when Jackson rushed up the

first three steps and said to the man, "Drop the rifle. And I mean now." The man complied.

Fargo stood up. He'd knocked his man over hard enough to leave him unconscious. He took the man's rifle and Colt and flung them out into the moonlit street.

After Fargo and Jackson had tamed the two, the bat-wings were unguarded and they proceeded inward. Wagon-wheel chandeliers, a mahogany bar, four tables for sitting with soiled doves or playing cards (your choice) . . . a pretty typical saloon by Fargo's lights.

Standish and Rhodes sat together at one of the tables. They'd apparently had only the two guards that Fargo and Jackson had taken out. They watched Fargo and Jackson approach. It was impossible to tell what they were thinking, let alone what they were planning.

Fargo heard Jackson gasp just a little. For a man who'd lived a long time under the iron hand of Theodore Standish, this confrontation had to be a bit like mocking a god. No wonder he'd gasped. But Fargo glanced at him and saw that Jackson had recovered quickly. The only sign of his anxiety was the way his jaw muscles bunched and un-bunched as the men approached the table.

Standish said, "Remind me to get some new guards." He looked funereal in a black suit, white shirt open at the collar. Normally a robust man, his face was pale and his eyes nervous. Rhodes didn't look much better.

"I'm putting both of you under arrest," Fargo said.

"If I'm not mistaken, you don't have a jail to put us in."

"The courthouse will do for now."

"And I'm not clear what the charges are."

"Murder, for one thing. Conspiracy, for another."

"I'm afraid I don't recall murdering anybody, Mr. Fargo."

"You ordered it done. Same thing."

"And you can prove this, of course."

"Won't be difficult."

Rhodes said, "I assume you know who you're talking to."

Fargo nodded. "Kind of hard not to in this town."

"I was with Mr. Standish all evening and I didn't see him or hear him order anybody to do anything."

"You'll be handcuffed right along with him. You'll have plenty of time to talk things over. Get your alibis straight."

"I resent your tone," Rhodes said.

"Stand up, Mr. Standish. I'll start with you."

And so it was joined. The unthinkable was about to happen. Somebody was arresting Theodore Standish. Right in the town he pretty much owned.

"And what if I don't?"

"Then I'll have to force you to stand up. And you won't like it."

Rhodes said, "This is preposterous."

"Shut up, Ty," Standish snapped. Then to Fargo: "I hope your Mr. Jackson understands that I have the power to foreclose on his farm and I intend to do so first thing in the morning."

"It's too late for that, Mr. Standish," Jackson said. "You can threaten all you want. I felt sorry for you because of Jane. Everybody liked her. But that didn't give you the right to do what you did tonight. Bryce Donlon deserved a fair trial."

"He murdered my daughter." Standish's face was suddenly an angry red. He brought a hammerlike fist down on the table. "I had a right to do whatever was necessary. And I don't give a damn whether you like it or not." He stood up abruptly, angling to the right, saying, "And I won't put up with any more from you two!"

And that was when he made his mistake. Feinting even more to the right, his left hand grabbing his holstered six-shooter, he managed to avoid the first shot Fargo fired. But now that he had the gun in his hand and was firing at Fargo—all this happening in a matter of a few seconds—he looked stunned, shocked that one bullet blasted open his forehead while another ripped open his throat.

He spun around, slamming into the wall behind him. He bounced off it almost comically and then fell without ceremony to the floor.

All Rhodes could summon was the same phrase over and over, "My God! My God! My God!"

23

After Tyler Rhodes had been secured in a small room in the courthouse, Fargo told Jackson to go on home and settle up things with his wife.

"I guess we've got a lot to talk about," Jackson said.

"I guess you do."

"I want her to know that I love Mark like if he was my own."

"She'll want to hear that."

"And that what happened in the past—" He shrugged. "I'm pretty sure she loves me, Fargo."

"Well, there's one way to find out." He smiled. "Now get the hell out of here."

For the next hour, as he sat in a comfortable chair he'd dragged out from one of the offices, the town paid Fargo their respects. The cook from the café brought him a fine steak dinner. A woman from one of the churches brought him two heavy woolen blankets. The librarian brought him two novels and three magazines.

This was the way to stand guard on a prisoner, Fargo thought. He might actually get some sleep tonight.

And he was about to doze off when he heard somebody knocking on the side door of the courthouse. Fargo's chair was right around the corner from the hall that led to the side entrance. He'd finished his meal and was getting lazy with the satisfaction of it and didn't especially want to get up, but what choice did he have?

Toting his Colt, he went to the door and saw through the glass the face of Frank Rhodes. He was here no doubt to argue that his father was a fine, upstanding man and

should be set free—for the good of not only the town but for all humanity—as soon as possible. Preferably, in the next five minutes.

"I can hear him snoring in there," Fargo said. "If you want to see him, come back in the morning."

"It's you I want to see, Mr. Fargo."

Only then did Fargo realize how disheveled and aggrieved Rhodes looked. None of the arrogance you might expect from a member of the Rhodes family. The eyes especially suggested some terrible calamity in the man's recent past. You saw men like this coming home from war. Haunted was the only appropriate word.

"Bryce died tonight."

"I know that, Mr. Rhodes."

Rhodes raised his head and stared directly into Fargo's eyes. "But what you don't know is that he didn't kill Jane."

"You're sure of that?"

"Very sure, Mr. Fargo. You see, I killed her."

They sat on the steps of the side entrance. Fargo kept the door open so he could hear any sound from inside. As Rhodes haltingly went through his story, Fargo kept rolling cigarettes and burning through them at a very quick rate.

"There's one thing you're leaving out, Rhodes."

"What's that?" the young man said miserably.

"For now I'll take your word that you killed her—but *why* did you kill her?"

"She broke off our engagement."

"Nobody mentioned that to me."

"She hadn't told anybody yet. She was waiting for church on Sunday to tell her friends."

The late-night sweetness of birds and breeze and silver moon settled in on the two men as they sat there in silence for a time.

"It's kind of funny."

"What is?"

"I can't even remember stabbing her. And that's why she broke it off with me. My drinking, I mean. I promised her I'd give up the bottle. She made me promise that the next time I got drunk I'd be honorable enough to tell her.

But I didn't, of course. I kept hiding it from her. I'd call on her in the early evening and then go to my home by myself and get drunk. The only way she found out was one night I stumbled on the way to the outhouse and put a gash in my forehead. I tried to convince her that I was sober when it happened. But she knew better. She had an aunt who was married to a drunkard, she told me. And even though he tried very hard to stay sober, he'd always fall off the wagon. Jane said she didn't want to have her children live a life like that, with everybody miserable all the time."

"Do you remember seeing Jane the night of the stabbing? You say you don't remember much about being in the alley—how did you even know she was in the alley?"

"I followed her from her house. We'd broken it off two nights before but I couldn't stop myself from going out there. The first night she stayed in. But the second night—I always hid behind a stand of trees down the lane—she went into town. I went to a saloon and got blind drunk. I don't remember how we connected. But I dimly remember following her. And then I kind of came to with blood all over my hands and arms and her laying in the alley at my feet. Then it all gets hazy. The next thing I remember clearly is waking up the next morning in my own bed. My father was in a rush to blame Donlon so the case would be closed right away."

"You're admitting to murder."

"I don't have much choice. I can't live with what I've done."

Fargo sighed. The night was so clean and enticing. He thought about Jane Standish. Yes, there was a girl murdered but there were other lives that were, for all practical purposes, about to be ended, too. Rhodes here and his father. And his mother. Jane had been right to call off the engagement. Rhodes deserved to be punished for killing the innocent girl. Violence took so many people down with it. That was one thing the dime novelists never dealt with.

"There's a room down the hall from your father. I'm putting you in there. I don't have to tell you not to try anything, do I?"

"I'm too tired to try anything. I'm just bone weary and right now I don't give a damn if I live or die. I really don't." He pushed his hands out. Fargo took his extra pair of handcuffs and cinched them on Frank Rhodes's wrists.

24

By midmorning, Fargo had found two men he felt he could trust to guard the Rhodeses. He sent a telegram to Carson City explaining the fire and the lack of an adequate place to hold prisoners. They wired back within the hour saying that they would agree to put the two prisoners up until such time as trials could be held. Fargo planned to put them on a train the following day and deliver them to the Carson City jail. Then he planned to ride the hell out of this state and not come back for a long, long time.

Exhausted as he was, he had a difficult time sleeping for an hour in his hotel bed because of the heat. Everything he touched felt corrosively hot. He slept for maybe twenty minutes, woke up and decided to hell with it. He went down the hall and got some fresh water and then bathed his torso, neck and face. He scraped away his day's growth with a razor that wouldn't cut butter. But a clean shirt, a few cigarettes and two cups of coffee at the café contrived to make him feel much better.

While he waited for his lunch, he felt most of the people in the place watching him. He glanced around occasionally. He saw a variety of expressions on the faces of the watchers. Some saw him as a hero; some saw him as a scoundrel; and some were simply curious about a man who had managed to kill Ted Standish and arrest not only one Rhodes, but both of them.

The food was good. Three eggs over easy, sliced potatoes, bread and raspberry jam and more fresh coffee.

He was just rolling a cigarette and finishing his coffee when a man walked directly to his table and said, "I'm one

of the fire brigade, Mr. Fargo. I found this in the rubble this morning. Except for a few scorch marks on the cover, it's still in good shape. Figured Grace probably brought it for Bryce to read. Must've been in his cell. Anyway, if you see her maybe you could give it to her."

The man was short, bald, chunky. But he had intelligent brown eyes and a reverent manner that Fargo appreciated after dealing with so many gunnies and crooks in this town.

"Thank you," Fargo said. "I'll see that she gets it."

After the man left, Fargo sat there finishing his cigarette and coffee. He looked at the cover of the novel occasionally. *Honorary Indian: A White Man's True Tale*. Fargo had to smile about that one. Anytime anybody under any circumstances advertised a book or a play or a magazine article as "true," there was a good chance it was anything but.

It was while he was standing up that he accidentally bumped the table and knocked the book on the floor. It was while he was bending over to pick it up that he saw that the book cover had been thrown back to the page that bore a handwritten inscription. It was while he was staring at the inscription that he realized who the real killer was.

"You sure you wouldn't like anything to drink, Skye?" Grace Donlon said after seating him in the living room of her comfortable home.

"No. I'm fine. Really."

She sat down in a chair facing his. She wore a white blouse. The only color on it was the brown of her nipples. Her red hair was pulled back today, emphasizing the perfection of her facial features, especially her somewhat arrogant but profoundly seductive mouth. But Fargo knew he couldn't let himself get distracted into any kind of sexual liaison.

He got up and walked across to her and handed her the book. "They found this in the rubble this morning. They thought you should have it. It's the book you brought Bryce last night."

"Oh, thank you," she said. Fargo knew that different people reacted differently to the death of a loved one. Some became hysterical. Others became emotionless, dead

in their own way. But when she took the book she made a sobbing sound so artificial he almost laughed at her. "God, I'm glad I was able to see him before he died." Her tears weren't authentic either. She had to squeeze them out of herself. "He was my life to me."

Fargo sat down again. "That's an awful nice inscription you wrote. Must've meant a lot to him."

She opened the book and looked inside. " 'To Bryce on his eighteenth birthday. Our folks would be so proud of you. Love, your sister, Grace.' " Then she paused, picked up something that had been laid inside. "What's this?"

"Piece of a note I found in the alley where Jane was killed. At first I wasn't sure that it had anything to do with her murder. But then this morning I looked at your inscription. It looked familiar for some reason. The handwriting, I mean. Then I remembered that scrap of paper I'd found in the alley. I compared the scrap to the inscription. Same handwriting. Identical, in fact. Even the same color ink. You must have to special-order that russet color."

"I'm not sure what you're saying here, Skye. But I certainly don't like your tone."

He stood up. "I'm arresting you for the murder of Jane Standish. You figured that most people would assume that Bryce killed her."

"But that's crazy. I loved Jane and I loved Bryce."

"That may be. But you loved money a lot more. With Bryce going to the gallows, you would inherit the entire estate your uncle left both of you. If you'd killed Bryce directly, people might get suspicious. But if it looked like he killed Jane— How'd you get her to meet you? You must've told her that you had something important to tell her. But it probably wasn't too hard. She trusted you. She thought you were friends."

She eased herself up from the chair. Walked slowly toward him. And then she was in his arms. He hadn't had time to resist. Or maybe he didn't want to resist. It was hard to know and for a long time there he didn't give a damn about anything except feeling the impulses that plush body awakened in him. He found his hands dropping to her buttocks, pulling her even tighter against his groin, so tight that they began a dance that was very much like copu-

lation. She was the scents of musk, perfume, clean hair and perfect flesh.

And then she was the sharp jab of metal. She'd pushed a derringer against his neck. "I'm going to get out of this town, Skye. And you're going to help me."

"You're overlooking something, Grace."

"I don't think so, Skye."

And that was when he jabbed her in the ribs with the Colt he'd eased from his holster some time ago.

"You bastard," she said.

"You can kill me, Grace, but I'll be taking you right along with me."

"You bastard."

Which she kept saying all the way to the courthouse, where he locked her up in the room that had been holding Frank Rhodes. She even continued to say it when he put her on the train with Tyler Rhodes the next morning, the train headed for Carson City and the prospect of a real jail cell.

LOOKING FORWARD!
**The following is the opening
section from the next novel in the exciting**
Trailsman **series from Signet:**

**THE TRAILSMAN #319
LOUISIANA LAYDOWN**

*New Orleans, 1860—smiling faces sometimes lie, as
the Trailsman learns in a city devoted to lying,
larceny and danger of every kind, including murder.*

Skye Fargo wrinkled his nose at the stench of the city and
ignored the cursing young man stumbling along in the wake
of his Ovaro stallion. Squinting his eyes to mere slits to
keep out the dust rising into the air, he put his heels to the
horse and felt the rope tied to his saddle horn tighten as
his prisoner tried to keep up.

Fargo's most recent trail had been a hard one, but the
bounty on the man he was bringing in would more than
make up for it. Billy "Dynamite" Briggs had robbed his
last train, and Fargo suspected that even if he escaped, he
wouldn't go very far. Being walked behind a strong horse
and a determined man hadn't been good for Billy's
constitution—he looked shamed and weak.

The brand-new Minneapolis and St. Louis train company

had offered $2,500 to the man who could bring Billy in to stand trial—they wanted him alive—and when Fargo had heard the news, he'd saddled his horse and started tracking. There wasn't much in the West that he hadn't been able to track down and while Billy was a bit more canny and elusive than many others had been, three weeks after he'd started, Fargo found him hiding out in a cave three days north of St. Louis.

Spotting the sign for the train station, Fargo paused and looked back at his prisoner. He *was* alive, but would probably have preferred to be dead. "Almost there, boy," Fargo said. "They might even let you sit down for a spell."

"Go to hell," Billy spat between breaths. "We coulda been partners, split the money and gone our separate ways. The reward wasn't worth as much as I offered you."

Fargo laughed coldly. "Nope, it wasn't. But that's justice, boy. It doesn't pay as well as crime, but a feller gets to sleep better at night."

"You're no lawman," Billy said, shaking his sweat-soaked, dirty blond hair out of his eyes. His hat was long since gone.

Fargo nodded. "And you're no dangerous criminal, but they'll pay me for you just the same." He spurred the Ovaro once more, forcing Billy to trot in order to keep up.

The noise at the main train station and offices was almost deafening—the M&StL mostly ran cargo, with some passengers, so there was all the racket of crates and cattle being loaded, along with the calls of conductors, families trying to get organized and the general chaos of the other nearby stations adding to the racket. The Ovaro laid his ears back and huffed. Fargo patted him on the neck as he climbed out of the saddle.

"We won't be here long, old boy," he said. "We'll take our reward and be on our way."

He untied the rope from the saddle horn and shortened the length in quick loops. "Come on, Billy," he said. "Let's get it over with." He gave the rope a quick tug and Billy stumbled forward.

"What's keeping you upright, boy?" Fargo asked. "Most men would be on their knees crying for mercy by now."

"Hate," Billy said, spitting into the street. "My mama didn't raise me to be a crybaby, neither. I'll come for you, Fargo, someday when you're sleeping peacefully because you're a law-abiding citizen." He spat again. "What bullshit."

Fargo could feel the waves of hate coming off him and knew the boy meant what he said. If he could come after him, he would. He stared hard at the bedraggled-looking boy before him. "You'll want to think might hard on that before you do. The railroad wanted you alive, boy, but if somehow you escape and come after me, you'll only get one thing"—he pulled his Colt smoothly from its holster and placed it directly in Billy's eye—"dead."

He slid the gun back into the holster and said, "Now shut up and move along. St. Louis may be a big city now, but it's still quick with its justice. I'd hate for you to be late to your own hanging." Fargo jerked on the rope and walked up the steps into the train office, pulling Billy along beside him.

The inside of the train office was dusty and hot. The shades were pulled down over the open windows, letting in the noise and the dirt and a humid spring wind, but that was about all. To the left was the ticket window, manned by a balding clerk who looked like he was on the edge of heatstroke, and to the right was a single door marked STATION OFFICE. Fargo knocked on it and when a sharp voice called out, "Enter," he did.

The man sitting behind the desk was hugely fat, with muttonchop whiskers that ran down the sides of his jowls in red wisps. He wore a full suit despite the heat and beads of perspiration lined his forehead. His face was flushed red and Fargo noted the bottle of Old Grand-Dad sitting on the desktop. Heat and whiskey weren't a good mix in Fargo's experience.

He glanced at the nameplate on the desk. "You're Mr. Waterstone?"

The man gave Fargo the once-over, taking in his battered

trail clothes and unshaven appearance. "I am," he said. "What do you want?"

Fargo gave the rope a quick yank, pulling Billy Briggs into the room. "The reward," he said smoothly. "This is Billy Briggs."

Waterstone's eyes lit up. "That's the best news I've heard all day!" he said. "What's your name, stranger?"

"Fargo," he said. "Skye Fargo." He reached into his coat pocket and pulled out the crumpled flyer, tossing it onto Waterstone's desk, then nudged Billy. "Speak up, boy."

"He's right," Billy said. "I'm the one you're looking for."

Waterstone leaned back in his chair, took a long sip from his glass and bawled, "Jacob! Get in here!"

Fargo listened as the old man from behind the ticket counter woke up from his heat-induced nap and scrambled across the station into the office. "Yes, sir, Mr. Waterstone?"

"Run down to the sheriff's office and bring him. Mr. Fargo here has just brought in a wanted fugitive."

The clerk nodded and headed off at a quick pace, moving his old legs faster than Fargo had imagined possible. He either wanted away from Waterstone, Billy Briggs, the heat or the boredom, but in any case, he moved fast for an old codger.

"This is just excellent news, Mr. Fargo," Waterstone said. "My employers will be most pleased and so will the sheriff, though I expect that he was hoping to cash in on the reward of two hundred and fifty dollars himself."

Fargo narrowed his eyes at the man. "What did you say?" he asked, his voice like steel.

"I . . . I said the sheriff was probably hoping to cash in on the reward himself."

"I heard that part," Fargo said. "I'm more interested in the amount. Did you say two hundred fifty?"

Waterstone nodded. "Yes, yes," he said. "It's all right here on the poster." He picked up the flyer and waved it in the air.

"Mister, you may think I'm nothing but an illiterate bounty hunter, but you better get your figures right in a

hurry. The reward posted by your company was two thousand five hundred dollars, and if you don't have it, then I'm afraid I'll just have to let poor Billy here go." Fargo's voice was calm, but his hand dropped smoothly to the butt of the Colt. "Or I'll have to take it out of you the hard way. Which do you prefer?"

Waterstone paled and quickly grabbed at the flyer, then made a show of looking it over. "Right you are, Mr. Fargo," he said. "My mistake. It *is* two thousand five hundred. There's no need for threats! The M&StL stands by its promises. Is a company draft acceptable?" He began rummaging through his desk.

Billy laughed. "Fargo, looks like you did a lot of work for damn little pay. You should've accepted my offer."

"Shut up, Billy," Fargo said, giving the rope a yank. He turned his attention back to Waterstone. "Cash," he said to the fat man. "I can wait while you run to the bank."

"I . . . Mr. Fargo, I will have to have the funds wired from Minneapolis. Our operating account here isn't large enough to cover that kind of expense." Waterstone raised his hands. "Please—you'll get your money. It should only take a couple of days at the most."

Fargo scowled at the man. "You know, Mr. Waterstone, when I found Billy here he had a sizable amount of money on him. Money he took from your trains. He even offered me a cut to just let him go." He gave another yank on the rope. "Guess you were right, Billy. Let's go divvy it up."

He turned and started out of the office, while behind him Waterstone let out a yelp. "Please, Mr. Fargo. One day! That's all it will take is one day, I swear."

Fargo looked back at the man. "All right," he said. "One day. I'll even let the sheriff take Billy into custody. But when I come back tomorrow afternoon . . . I expect to be paid. Every penny. If I'm not, things are going to get downright ugly for you. Understood?"

Waterstone nodded. "Yes, sir, Mr. Fargo. You'll get every penny tomorrow afternoon."

Fargo nodded and said, "I better." He turned back to Billy. "Let's go, boy. We'll wait for the sheriff outside."

"You're a fool, Fargo," Billy said. "You ain't going to see one dime."

Fargo laughed. "I wouldn't worry on it too much if I were you, Billy. I'll get what I'm due for the work I've done—I always get paid what I'm due."

Billy looked at the hardened features of the man before him, then said, "I bet you do. But sooner or later, everyone gets shorted; everyone lays down."

"Not me," Fargo said, yanking him onto the boardwalk to await the sheriff. "Not ever."

The next afternoon, Waterstone had come through with the money and Fargo had gotten himself some clean clothes, a shave and a haircut. He'd also taken the time to buy himself a fine steak dinner with a good whiskey and a clean bed to sleep in that night.

He almost felt like a new man—and he didn't want that feeling to end.

There was no pressing reason for him to get back out on the trail, and St. Louis was filled to bursting with people talking about New Orleans and how decadent it had become. Luxurious brothels, expensive gambling, horse racing, duels and more occurred on a nearly continual basis. For that reason, Fargo decided it might be an interesting place to visit.

Maybe he'd do well gambling and increase the size of his poke and maybe not, but either way, it was someplace new and if he didn't like it, he could always move on. In fact, Fargo knew that eventually he *would* move on—that was his nature—but in the meantime, he had enough money to see at least a glimpse of how the rich city folk lived.

He led the Ovaro down to the docks of the Mississippi River, where he booked passage for himself and the horse to New Orleans aboard a riverboat. The ship was good-sized and boasted private cabins and a fine saloon, complete with a fully stocked bar and humidor. Once he'd secured his horse and put his belongings away, Fargo headed

for the dining room to wait for the boat to leave in the evening.

He wanted another good meal and perhaps a game of cards before calling it a night.

The waitress—a red-haired wench who clearly had more cleavage than sense, but a nice smile and a firm rear end— took his order and hinted that more services might be available after the boat closed down for the evening.

Fargo grinned and told her he'd keep it in mind, then sipped his whiskey while he waited for his dinner: pot roast with new potatoes and carrots, cornbread, and apple pie for dessert. For a man who'd lived most of his life on trail rations or worse, it was a damn fine meal and he enjoyed it thoroughly before strolling toward the saloon to see if he could find a good game of poker that would hold his interest.

The main saloon and gambling room of the riverboat was a stark contrast to its cargo hold. Appointed in leather and dark green hues, it encouraged privacy at most of its tables, while the center of the room was dominated by card tables, well lit and attended by serving girls who kept the booze flowing freely.

Fargo wandered around the room, content to watch for a bit until he found a table he liked. Eventually, a seat opened as one man folded his cards in disgust and walked away. "Not my night," he said as he passed by. "Maybe your luck will be better."

"I hope so," Fargo said, sitting down.

The dealer eyed his plain clothing. "The buy-in for this table is one hundred dollars, sir," he said. "Perhaps there are other tables that would be more to your liking."

Resisting the urge to punch the pompous ass in the face, Fargo pulled the money out of his vest. "I'm in," he said, keeping his voice even. "And you'd do better not to judge a book by its cover."

"Yes, sir," the dealer said, taking the money and quickly handing Fargo his chips. He glanced around the table once more and added, "The game is five-card draw, nothing wild. Ante is five dollars, no top bet."

Fargo flicked a five-dollar chip forward and studied the other five players as they anted up. Most of the men were nondescript, but there was one who caught his attention immediately. Immaculately dressed and groomed, he appeared to be a city gentleman, with long sideburns and dark brown hair streaked liberally with gray. His suit was pressed and neat, his tie properly done up. *He could be a professional,* Fargo thought.

The dealer pushed out the first set of cards and Fargo glanced at his—a pair of eights, an ace of clubs, and junk.

"Bets, gentlemen?" the dealer said.

Fargo checked first, waiting to see what the other players—especially the potential professional—would do.

Three players folded in a row, then the next one, an old man, said, "I'm in for ten," and put the chips on the table.

The well-dressed man called quietly, placing his chips on the table.

"Mr.—?" the dealer asked.

"Fargo," he replied. "Skye Fargo." He looked once more at the other two players and nodded. "I'm in." He added his own chips to the growing pile.

There was already more money on the table than most cowpunchers would see in six months of work and even though he was flush at the moment, Fargo briefly thought about all the times he hadn't been and wondered if he'd be better off saving his poke for a rainy day than spending it on gambling and booze. Then he grinned to himself. *Better to live well while I can. Hard days will come whether I'm flush or not.*

"Cards, gentlemen?" the dealer asked.

"I'll take two," Fargo said, keeping his eights and his ace. The dealer spun the cards out.

"Three," the old man said, taking his cards.

"I'll stand pat," the well-dressed man said.

The dealer nodded. "Yes, sir, Mr. Parker." He looked at Fargo. "Your bet, sir?"

Fargo wondered if the man was bluffing or had simply been dealt a strong hand. "Check," Fargo said.

"Sir?" the dealer asked the old man.

Watching him, Fargo noticed that the old man's hands were holding his cards tightly, twisting his wrist almost inward. *He's going to bet,* Fargo thought.

"Twenty-five," he said, sliding the chips forward.

It was almost impossible to see, but Fargo had spent many years relying on his instincts and his ability to see what others could not. The *old man* was the professional—a professional cheat. He slipped a card out of his sleeve with one hand, even as he moved his chips forward, using them as a minor distraction.

"I'll see your twenty-five," Mr. Parker said, "and raise you twenty-five." He put his chips forward.

More than anything, Fargo hated a cheat. Poker was a game of skill and chance, but no one had a chance if someone at the table was cheating. Still, other than his own eyes—and he was brand-new at the table—he had no proof.

"Interesting," he said. "It's fifty to me, right?"

"Yes, sir," the dealer said.

Fargo leaned forward, watching the old man intently. People who were flush didn't usually cheat. People who were desperate did. "Let's make it," he said, reaching into his vest, "five hundred dollars." He put the cash on the table.

The old man stared at him, his Adam's apple bobbing as he swallowed hard. "That's a lot of money, mister," he said.

Fargo nodded. "It is," he agreed. "Call, raise or fold."

"You're bluffing," he said. "I'll allow you to retract the bet. You can't afford to lose that much money."

Fargo grinned. "Maybe," he said. "But I haven't looked at my draw cards yet. And I don't bet unless I'm sure of winning."

His hands trembling, the old man counted his chips. "I can call to . . . one hundred seventy-five," he said. "It's all I've got left."

"Fine," Fargo said. "Make the call."

The old man slid the last of his chips forward, and once again, took a card from his sleeve. *He must have half a deck up there,* Fargo thought. *He's loaded now.*

The man called Parker sat up a little straighter and

glanced at Fargo. "You aren't what you appear to be," he said. "That's a very large bet for a man who hasn't seen his draw cards. Are you trying to force a laydown, sir?"

"No," Fargo said. "But I'm going to make an example of our friend here in just a moment." He gestured at the pile of chips. "Your bet, Mr. Parker," he said.

Parker looked at him intently, then shrugged. "Poker is as much about the players as the cards," he said. "I have a feeling about you." He laid his cards down. "Fold."

"Smart," Fargo said.

"Gentlemen, your cards please," the dealer said.

Fargo showed his pair of eights and his ace.

The cheat grinned and laid down his three jacks and two queens. "Full house, Mr. Fargo," he said. "Let's see your other cards."

Fargo shook his head. "I'd rather see the rest of yours first," he said, lowering his hand down to his Colt.

"I've shown all of mine," the old man said.

"Not those," Fargo replied. "I mean the ones in your sleeve."

"You're accusing me of cheating!" he cried, leaping to his feet. "How dare you!"

"Easy," Fargo said, pointing with his left hand. "Mr. Parker, take a look at the tip of his left sleeve. I believe that this gentleman's luck has just run out."

Parker leaned forward, then suddenly seized the man's arm, yanking out several cards in a flurry. "You are a cheat!" he said.

The old man whipped his right arm forward, a small derringer appearing as if by magic. The room went silent. "Back off, Parker," he said. "At this range, even a derringer can kill you."

Fargo slipped the Colt free of its holster, keeping it pointed at the man beneath the table. "Put down the peashooter, mister," he said. "Put it down and walk away or they're going to carry you out of here on a slab."

The old man lunged forward, pointing the little gun at Parker's head. "Shut up, Fargo. I'm getting out of here." He shoved at his hostage. "Get going."

"Hold it, mister," Fargo snapped. "Don't make it worse than it already is."

He noted that for a man in a life-threatening situation, Parker seemed calm. *Time for another gamble,* he thought.

The old man turned back to snarl something more and Fargo shouted, "Move, Parker!"

Parker lunged out of the way and Fargo cut loose with the Colt. The slugs took the old man in the knees and he screamed as he fell.

Fargo jumped to his feet and aimed the Colt at the prone man, who was moaning and clutching at his legs. He put a boot down on the derringer. "See there," Fargo said, after the shouting had died down. "I guess the kid was right. Sooner or later, everyone lays down. Guess it was your turn."

Parker got to his feet and nodded at Fargo. "You saved my life, sir," he said. "The least I can do is buy you a drink."

"Why not?" Fargo asked, picking up his draw cards, then tossing them down in disgust. "That hand was terrible anyway."

No other series packs this much heat!

THE TRAILSMAN

**Available wherever books are sold or at
penguin.com**

National Bestselling Author
RALPH COMPTON

NOWHERE, TEXAS
THE SKELETON LODE
DEATH RIDES A CHESNUT MARE
WHISKEY RIVER
TRAIN TO DURANGO
DEVIL'S CANYON
SIX GUNS AND DOUBLE EAGLES
THE BORDER EMPIRE
AUTUMN OF THE GUN
THE KILLING SEASON
THE DAWN OF FURY
DEATH ALONG THE CIMMARON
RIDERS OF JUDGMENT
BULLET CREEK
FOR THE BRAND
GUNS OF THE CANYONLANDS
BY THE HORNS
THE TENDERFOOT TRAIL
RIO LARGO
DEADWOOD GULCH
A WOLF IN THE FOLD
TRAIL TO COTTONWOOD FALLS
BLUFF CITY
THE BLOODY TRAIL
WEST OF THE LAW
BLOOD DUEL
SHADOW OF THE GUN
DEATH OF A BAD MAN